THE

TALENTED

Xth

By

Gibran Tariq

Author's Foreword

In early 1998, after arriving in the federal pen at Atlanta to begin my sentence for drug trafficking, I was eager to start writing. However, I couldn't of think of a challenging topic until one evening, I read an article about Matthew Shepard, a young college student, who was tortured and killed because he was gay. The article touched me, and the senseless inhumanity of the murder disturbed me as I detest discrimination of any sort. This young man was killed because he was assumed to be powerless and invisible, so none of the characters in this novel have names to protest powerlessness and being invisible. PEACE

C H A P T E R   1

Spring 1960

"**W**ake up! Wake up! Go to the car!"

It was my Mother. Frantic and hysterical, she loudly roused both my brother and me from a fitful, restless sleep.

"You little motherfuckers better get up. Now!"

In these moments, Mother didn't allow us the pleasure of full consciousness. All she wanted was enough wakefulness to either induce movement or to recognize pain. I dodged a swift backhand. My younger brother, not so lucky, was hit with a perfumed gloved fist. He yelped in pain, now fully awake. We, my brother and I, hit the floor, a blur of rehearsed motion.

"You niggers mighty slow for some reason this morning," Mother barked. "Don't make me get my belt."

The basic truth about these early morning occurrences was that nothing else, at that unholy time of morning, was more important than speed. Over time, my brother and I had grown quicker and more time efficient, but this morning, everything seemed much more urgent; decidedly more threatening.

"I'm warning y'all."

I stuffed both legs into my pants at the same time, and no sooner had I buttoned them at the waist than Mother was slamming a tri-colored tee shirt over my head, peeling my ears away from my head, and pressing my nose flat against my face.

The tee shirt smelled fresh.

Seconds later, we were out of the door, standing in the hot, sticky darkness, and for the first time in my life, I instinctively felt there was no scarier place for me to be than with my Mother

I never knew why but the stark, unyielding darkness always made Mother's black sedan appear much smaller.

Mother handed the keys to my brother and the two of us dashed through the darkness to the car. Mother moved at a much slower pace, standing still in the garish glow from the night light on the front porch while she smoothed her tight dress down over her too wide hips. She adjusted the wide, red belt, and touched her hair. Satisfied with her iridescent perfection, she got into the car, and we drove off.

It was three a.m. on a Sunday, and Mother had just found out where her husband was, and who he was sleeping with.

By most estimates, there was something incredibly extraordinary about what was getting ready to happen. I just didn't know what it was. Nonetheless, it was so palpable that my heart felt crammed inside my throat. I couldn't think so there was no precise way I could judge between was what real and what wasn't. Trapped in this netherworld, I wanted to try on the notion of bravery, and tell my Mother to stop the damned car, and to drive us to a place more sane than where she was now headed......wherever that was.

Every time I attempted to voice my studied objection to my Mother's madness, I learned, with no help, save the Divine, that sometimes bravery equaled foolishness.

In the back of my Mother' Buick, I also learned, unaided, when to distinguish the two, but what startled me most of all, though, was the unerring knowledge that this was not the time for either.

I remained silent.

And for the next two hours, Mother drove.

Turning down a dirt road, white alabaster dust swelled up around the body of Mother's speeding Buick, adding to the bizarre nature of the oncoming doom.

My brother was asleep.

Glancing into the car's interior mirror, the only feature I recognized on Mother's beautiful face was an animated 'don't-give-a-damn' smirk. It was fixed there, frighteningly oversized, providing her olive eyes with a vacant thunder that forced me to look away.

How could I challenge this reigning pressure in my head? It was fixed there, like my Mother's smirk.

The threat was so deeply imprinted on my brain that I felt that whenever *what-came-next* presented itself to Mother, it would force me into a rebirth-------or a total death. Suddenly, I didn't care to have anything swiped out of or from my young life, and although this was a brand new idea, I could predict that somehow my Mother had better come out on top. Or else.

In the meantime, the black Buick sped toward destiny, and we silently drove on until more than half the sky had hemorrhaged with a pale, steel grey light.

The house was egg-shell white.

"Black assed dog," Mother whispered, barely audible.

I vaguely wondered if she was referring to the mutt outside, or the man, her husband, inside.

"Dog!" she uttered more loudly, then with a high degree of certainty added. "That nigger is coming home with me, and nothing is going to get in my way."

We left the safety of the car.

A quarter of the way to the front door, Mother's husband appeared on the front porch. His creased, unsmiling face offered an unlimited number of possibilities, none of which benefited our strategic vulnerability.

"You amaze me," Mother's husband said.

"Come home, nigger." There was sternness in Mother's voice.

"Hmm," her husband muttered, scratching his goatee.

I shuddered, knowing that anything less than a jubilant yes would invite a full-blown crisis because Mother did not seem humored by any of the possibilities that "Hmm" presented.

Mother moved forward a step or two, advancing until her heel got caught on a rock, causing her to stumble awkwardly. She stopped. "And what kind of stupid answer is that? Hmm."

Fixed with the difficulty of explaining, her husband invested considerable time in his answer. "It means there are other options."

"Such as?"

Mother's husband became instantly aggressive as he nodded his head towards the door. "Her."

6

At this point, Mother kicked off her heels. She snarled viciously. "Bring the bitch out so I can kick her ass."

For a brief time, the silence jockeyed back and forth between them, abruptly ending only when a woman appeared out of the shadows cast by the darkness behind the doorway, and in one angry leap was at my Mother's throat.

Immediately, I sensed that this not-so-gentle physical introduction of this strange, new woman friend of my Mother's husband was crucial to our welfare as a family unit, so jumping in to assist Mother seemed to be the most important decision I could make at the moment although my biggest concern was what Mother's husband would do.

Soon, I found out.

"Get back, you lil, snot-nosed punk." He cuffed me upside the head. "What makes you think you done earned the right to interfere in grown folks biz'ness?"

"That's my Mama," I protested.

That fact seemed to amaze Mother's husband. "You think I don't know who that ho is, nigger. You better git yo' puny, little ass somewhere." He beamed. "These bitches battling for bragging rights."

Despite my interest in the outcome of this battle royale, I was not overly inspired watching Mother rumble. From the instant the fight started, both women exhibited unreasonable amounts of savage, animal fierceness. They were exchanging death blows.

"This is not just for me," Mother's husband remarked somberly. "It's for all of us because when this is over, we'll know, without doubt, which bitch is the best bitch."

Initially, I was reluctant to dampen his joy, but there was no other way to communicate the difficulty I had understanding his reasoning, so I flew into him, both arms flailing. "You black-assed, no-account cock-sucker." (I had heard Mother say that.)

He slapped me down. I jumped back up. The two women continued fighting.

Having anticipated that I couldn't whip Mother's husband, I was not badly traumatized by the fact that I could scarcely remember my name, or who my brother was. Mother, however, remained crystal clear to me, only now I couldn't tell if she was winning or losing. I was distraught.

By this time, Mother's violent campaign to win what her husband had called "bragging rights" was almost halted by what appeared to be a left haymaker. Mother dropped to the ground like a sack of rotten potatoes. I was doubly distraught.

Mother fell surprisingly hard, and I'll continue to believe that only some sort of para-military training could have allowed Mother to move so swiftly. She performed a marginally cute tuck and roll maneuver before lithely springing upright. Then she met the other woman two steps away from where she had fallen, and faking a short hook to the bitch's gut, grabbed her in a headlock.

Mother squeezed.

The other woman howled in pain which was the appropriate response to the brutal chokehold she now found herself in.

I encouraged Mother. "Harder, squeeze harder. Pop her neck."

Winning, or at least being on a winning team, is great for the spirit, and I experienced tremendous relief. Mother was winning. I happily slapped my brother on the back. "Look at Mother," I gushed. "She gonna break that heifer's neck."

In my case, my victory celebration was earnestly premature. I stared in horror as Mother was upended and slammed to the ground with the other woman landing squarely on top. None of Mother's favored punches and claw-holds seemed to offer much protection from the furious attack of the other woman. Mother was punched drunk. I mostly avoided watching this unflattering spectacle of my Mother's inability to defend herself. It made me uncomfortable to realize that whatever this defeat ushered in, it would mean that Mother would be at the bottom of the pecking order as far as her husband was concerned. This would, no doubt, make my life miserable.

"Ladies, ladies," Mother's husband intoned, peeling one woman off the other. "That's enough." He kissed the other woman on the cheek. You won." He stared at Mother disdainfully. "Damn, bitch, you sho' can't love me much, fighting like that. You could have stayed at home and spared yourself this ass-whupping if you wasn't going to fight no better than that." He helped Mother off the ground. "Damn, bitch, what was you thinking about?"

Mother was silent.

"I like winners," her husband said, "and you know that."

"But she's not the better woman."

Mother's husband frowned. "She won, fair and square."

"But can she fuck better than me?"

"Hmm." Mother's husband smiled slyly.

8

"Well, can she?" Mother purred. "Fucking is what make a woman a real winner."

Sometimes, it is best to leave well enough alone, and not to go any further down the road to perdition when the signs are clear that, more than likely, disaster   awaits. For some particular reason, Mother's husband didn't see fit to heed any warnings of any sort. And why should he, considering the opportunity that had now evolved from the ashes of such pre-meditated violence? How often was it that a man, of no special talent, could wrest such a wonderful surprise from the mayhem he had just witnessed?

"You know something, bitch," Mother's husband said to her. "In all my life, I ain't never even considered that, you know, what makes a bitch a good bitch other than the fact that she do all the shit I tell her to do, and when she gets finished doing that, to find other good shit to do for me that I ain't even thought about." He rubbed his chin. "Maybe, I just been taking good pussy for granted."

"Now, might be a good time to get schooled," Mother rasped.

The other woman huffed and puffed. "The only thang that nigger gonna find out is that he a fool if he don't stay right here---with me."

"Ladies, ladies," Mother's husband ordered. "Let's take this to the bedroom."

Less than one hour later, the county coroner pronounced Mother's husband dead. Apparently, too much of a good thing is not a good thing. Mother and the other woman fucked him to death, providing him with a massive heart attack.

"What a way to go," the mild-mannered, middle-aged coroner rasped after checking out the physical assets of the two women involved in the orgy. "Damn, what a way to go!"

CHAPTER 2

The first thing I noticed was that, at first, I was too embarrassed to be ashamed of it. Even though I was young, I knew that if it kept getting stronger, it would be a tricky, hard-to-hide secret. And then it would be a problem. A damned big one

Every few days following the fever of knowing, I would look into the mirror to see if my face or body showed any tell-tale signs of the physical betrayal I assumed would be coming, but so far---so good.

Other than the fact that I possessed this damning insider's tip about myself, my life hauled ass toward juvenile oblivion. Fortunately, the world my brother and I inhabited was not remade by the addition of The Other Woman in our lives. She was Mother all over again, so it was simply business as usual.

Both women lives were powered by the faint praise from the other, and their greatest ambition was to become even more alike. Their special complementary treatment of each other left very little rewards for my brother and me, but based on what all the other kids close by had or got, we were normal. Except for my secret!

The first time I exhibited my helplessness to resist the particular taste of my "coming" preference, I severely wounded a young girl. It had all started out as an innocent childhood game that almost became a murder. Anyway, it should have been obvious what our roles should have been, and it was to everyone---except me! In fact, it should never have occurred to me that there existed, for me, any other alternative. But I had this terrible secret, remember?

Why did I want to be Mommy?!

In a sane world, it can always be relied upon that when children play Mommy and Daddy, the little girl plays Mommy; the little boy plays daddy. *Always.* This was an universal law of childhood, but, for me, that day, it seemed so unnatural, so cruel that roles couldn't be switched at will.

I didn't want to be Daddy!

I wanted to be Mommy!

My young female playmate was startled, greatly upset. This was a new concept too her; revolutionary. I sold the idea hard, oozing charm, grabbing her skinny arm, and looking deeply into her confused, brown eyes.

"How 'bout it?"

"No!" she screamed. No! No! No!"

I bashed her head in with a tree limb.

And she was just my first victim.

Despite the early evidence, both Mother and the Other Woman believed desperately in the politics of sex. Their entire lives were nothing, if not, a sensual testament to the endurance and character of fucking, and it would break their hearts if they ever met a man who didn't exist to find good pussy, or a young boy who wouldn't eagerly take up the quest.

SURPRISE!

One of the first thing I learned to do after learning how to disguise my weakness and attractions for girly things was to lie. First to myself. Then to others.

Since I clearly understood, at this young age, that there would be no reasonable way for me to transform this weakness into an opportunity, I wouldn't take credit for anything it made me do. The blade of the guillotine was much too sharp.

I didn't have the slightest idea what best prepared a man to be 'different' but in October when I was sentenced to probation, I noted that punishment was the primary weapon.

The little girl and her family moved away.

11

Being on probation put me in a better position to understand myself because it provided me with a mentor. My probation officer was 'different' as well. This was my Head-Start. From him, I would be introduced to the genesis of an ideological purity that would change my life. Crime had done the seemingly impossible, bringing me face-to-face with a Messiah.

I don't recall any notion of fear as I looked at my sleeping brother. He was fast asleep, and there were no visible signs that he would awake any time soon. After a few seconds, the intense melodrama of what I was about to do made my eyelids flutter. Slowly, I inched closer to my brother, and when within arm's length, I nudged him gently. Still, no sign of wakefulness.

Drawing closer, I invented a game. I silently slid my body a bit to the right of my brother, dismissing my sinful intention, and when I had sufficiently whisked them out of view, I quietly peeled back the covers under which my brother snuggled peacefully.

I laid there stiff and frozen, openly gazing at the nubile, youthful body of my baby brother. And then I was overcome with the almost overpowering desire to touch him even though I knew I had not earned the clear-cut right to disrespect him in such an unchristian fashion Suddenly, I pondered what my reaction would be if I did so because I figured that 'sissiness' would be an immediate decree once I made the decision to end my curiosity. The ugly process of trying to prove myself wrong toyed with me.

It was almost midnight, but by now, all my primary doubts or regrets were gone, and then it came to me in a flash. I gazed over my left shoulder at my side of the bed, and inwardly, I wished it hadn't come to this. This truth was bittersweet, a hard pill to swallow but I digested it unnervingly well. *And then I touched my brother!*

Some few nights later, at approximately sometimes before dawn, I awoke drenched in sweat. I rolled over, quickly sitting up in the middle of the bed, and yanking the light cord, the tiny room exploded with light. I instantly felt better, but not relieved. Ever since probation, I had grown accustomed to sleepless nights and unanswered questions.

Could it be true?
Was there such a thing as The Talented Tenth?

CHAPTER 3

Within a year of my murder attempt, Mother was in the ideal position of being "nigger rich". Her restaurant was booming and becoming even more prosperous. (She had opened it right after the death of her husband, using the money left from the insurance policy).

In addition, the Other Woman turned out to be an excellent seamstress, and in no time was dressing all the more fashionable women in town. Mother had loaned her the money to pay for a small building around the corner from the family restaurant, and it too had blossomed.

Soon, we were rolling in dough.

Unlike other parts of the city where men were unemployed, the women angry, and the children illiterate, our community suddenly became middle class and fancy.

Ironically, at the same time, various cities only a stone's throw further South were gaining a reputation for racism and intolerance, but none of this mattered to Mother who fought hard to assimilate all of us into a dream that only she could see, and even though our lives were a far cry better than what anyone could normally expect for a family of blacks, Mother was not content. She wanted more. And more.

None of us in the house knew where Mother had inherited this taste for the good life. Her parents and their parents had been dirt poor, so maybe it was the fear of poverty that kept her moving. Anyway, it invested her with a charismatic arrogance, and a permanent disgust for those less fortunate than she was. Mother hated poor people, especially poor, black ones.

"Poor niggers make all the rest of us look bad," she preached.

Although everyone in town knew of Mother's dislike of the poor, not many realized just how serious it was until a ragged, dusty man entered the restaurant, and misjudged Mother.

"Miss," he begged. "I'm starving. Can you please spare me a meal?" His eyes were pleading, desperate.

Mother was lethally incensed. "Get out, beggar," she screamed. "How dare you come in her and insult my paying customers. Now get out and stay out."

"But, please, Miss. Just a little something. I haven't eaten in------."

"I don't give a damn if you ever eat again." Mother was outraged. "Now, get out!"

But as the seconds passed, the man barely moved from the place where he stood, and the tension increased. And to the surprise of Mother, the dirty beggar drew his old tattered coat around him grandly, and stood as proudly as a Hebrew king, and pointed a bony finger at Mother.

"*Bitch!*"

The word hung in the air so long there was no immediate repercussions, and the word probably would have hung there until doomsday, but perhaps out of the inability to leave well enough alone, the man repeated the curse.

"*Bitch!*"

This time Mother showed no signs of hesitation. She shot the man dead, and thirty minutes later, the cops arrested her.

Off to jail, Mother went.

Within days of her arrest, Mother was moved to the local hospital's mental ward because The Other Woman thought it would be easier on Mother this way. She still had to get a bond since the Grand jury had returned an indictment for 1st degree murder.

Of all the things Mother had done in her life, this was different. She had sometimes neglected my brother and me, had always slept with a wide assortment of gentlemen friends, very seldom resisted a fight with other women, but she had never killed before. I was in a state of shock though my baby brother appeared only mildly amused.

When we were permitted to visit Mother on the 'nut ward', I was surprised that confinement had not transformed her. She was still stern, uncompromising, and very sexy. Everything that Mother did, she treated as a success, so even under these dire conditions, she made it look as though there was something to celebrate. No one else, however, felt even remotely triumphant.

"Always keep smiling until the bottom falls out," Mother scolded us, but after giving thought to that remark added. "Never let the bottom fall out." She smacked her lips. *"Never."*

The bottom fell out. And it was classic.

You see, Mother's *'don't-worry-be-happy-and-keep-smiling'* philosophy was based on one single fact alone. That fact: She had good pussy, and that men would do anything to get some. The guard assigned to make sure Mother stayed put was one such man. None of his law enforcement training, nor his Christian ethics, if he possessed any, could or would do any good when they collided with the chance to fuck Mother.

Trusting in the process, Mother disabled him sexually until doing his sworn duty became dispensable, and Mother became indispensable, and on the same day that an all-white jury had convicted her, and the judge had sentenced her, Mother formed a huge void in their plans. She escaped and took the guard with her!

We disappeared like slaves running to get out of Egypt, and within days were somewhere else.

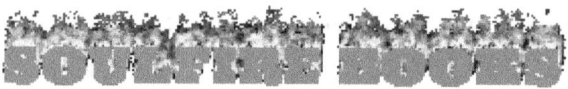

After a few months of freedom, Mother's 'full-bodied' spirit of rebellion returned. At least, that's what she wrote to The Other Woman, who stayed behind to manage the family businesses. Mother's new boyfriend said it was much more. He boldly accused Mother.

"Yo' damn pussy so hot it won't stay in your draws," he said. "After all I done done for you, this is the thanks I get. Nowadays, it seems like the only damn time your legs closed is when I want to get between them."

"You fucks enough, nigger, so don't give me that shit 'bout you ain't getting enough ass." She purred. "Ain't it stiil good to you?"

16

"Hell yeah, it's good, woman. You good and damn well know it."

"Then what's the problem, baby."

"I want it all for myself. Is that too much to ask? I just stand the thought of having to share you."

"They can't use it up," Mother cooed. "There'll always be some left over just for you."

"*You slut!*" he exploded. "Don't you understand that I don't want no second-hand pussy."

Mother pouted. "That door ain't locked, motherfucker."

"I-I left my wife and children for you----"

"Don't forget," Mother added, "the part about your damn job. If you gonna do it, just as well get it all in."

Frustrated, the boyfriend slapped Mother. "You may not know it now or like it later, but you gonna stop giving away pussy. Ain't nobody getting none---but me."

Mother cursed. "Fuck you, you bastard." She snarled hotly. "You don't own me or my pussy, so you can take that notion and throw it in the ocean."

"You-you think this some kind of motherfucking joke. You think I'm telling you some kind of nursery rhyme or some fairytale bullshit." Mother's boyfriend was angry and aggressive. "Starting right this damn moment, you done gave up your last shot of ass to outside motherfuckers, and the only two things you can do 'bout it is either to learn to love it or enroll yo' red ass in a convent."

Mother mimicked disbelief. "But, baby, you can't------."

"Shut up, bitch, and take off that dress."

"Wha-----."

"And get yo' fine, naked ass in bed."

"But----."

"Bitch, we either fucking or fighting. Don't make me no never-mind which way it go. I got some steam to let off, and the way I feel right now, I'll get just as much satisfaction knocking you out as knocking yo' pussy loose."

"Okay, big daddy," Mother conceded, "you win. From now on, you ain't gonna be having no more trouble out of me." She giggled naughtily. "I didn't know this pussy was that good too you." She blushed. "Now, that I know just how much you loves this pussy, can't no other nigger get none. Nigger, Im gonna whup this pussy on you like I ain't

17

never done before, but first, I'm gonna take my fine, red ass into the kitchen and fix you a big, ol' pork chop dinner. Then we can fuck, okay?'

"Now, you talking like you done finally got some sense. Now, go fix me a plate, bitch."

"I hear you, daddy." Mother dashed into the kitchen, giggling.

"And don't be putting no pussy juice in my food, bitch."

"Nigger," Mother giggled, "you so crazy."

Later, as Mother's boyfriend ate, both my brother and I agreed that he looked funny, trying to be tough, and choking to death at the same time. Mother had poisoned his pork chops. His dying was intense, a wide array of various facial contortions and spasms, each one more gaspingly horrible than the one that preceded it. It was, for sure, death by degree, in stages.

On its face, the death of Mother's boyfriend should have placed us in a very uncomfortable situation, but Mother had no tolerance for unpredictability, so even before the man who had deserted his family, and had sprung her from jail had gasped his last breath, the threshold of what to do next had been crossed.

Mother left and shortly returned with a pair of men, blood brothers, who removed the dead body. They disposed of the man, and when they returned, they went into the bedroom with Mother.

The brothers spent the night and Mother made sure they enjoyed themselves immensely. The night flew by, but it was during breakfast that the situation got a wee bit more, shall I say, complicated.

"As much as it would please me," Mother declared innocently, "but I can only make room for one of you in my life."

Breakfast was forgotten.

With that vital announcement, Mother had signaled an abrupt end to all the childhood joy there had been growing up together, and being related by blood. There could now easily be unsurmountable problems since nothing was as sought after than good pussy, and both brothers knew it. For the two of them, this was unprecedented because it was something that couldn't be settled by seniority. The younger one wouldn't stand for that. It could not be settled by youth because the older brother would not accept that. This was the penultimate moment for them.

"How we gonna handle this?" one asked.

"Ain't but one way."

"One way?" Tension filled the air.

"That's correct, nigger, one way."

"Yeah?"

"Yeah!"

"What's that way, fool"

"Simple."

"Yeah?"

"Yeah!"

"What is it, then, nigger?"

"The motherfucker with the biggest dick wins."

"Hell naw, nigger."

"Why the fuck not?"

"It ain't fair."

"How you figure that; ain't fair?"

"You must really think I'm stupid or something, don't you? You the oldest, so quite naturally your dick might be bigger since it done had mo' time to grow."

"So, what you wanna do, scared-assed nigger. I ain't got all morning to be fucking 'round with you."

"If you ask me, that don't leave but one thang."

Both brothers stood.

"Wait," Mother shrieked, "no bloodshed." She had never been squeamish before. "Sit down."

Both men plopped down into their chairs, and Mother tossed a deck of playing cards onto the kitchen table. "High card wins."

After a grueling twenty second debate over who was going to shuffle the cards, it was finally decided that only Mother could touch the cards.

The brothers sweated as the shuffling of the cards sounded sinister as Mother deftly mixed the cards up, the swooshing sound amplified in the stillness of the room. You could hear a pin drop. Fear registered on the faces of both men. This was for good pussy; winner take all. Finally, a single blue-backed card was placed face down before each brother.

"Turn over your cards," Mother instructed.

Neither brother made a move. Both appeared transfixed by the sure knowledge that life, as they knew it, would no longer exist once the cards were turned over. They knew, of a certainty, that the cards would bless one of them and curse the other.

19

"Your cards, gentlemen," Mother prodded. "Turn them over." When both men sat motionless, Mother yelled for my brother and me. Racing into the kitchen, not knowing what to expect, our Mother stood one of us beside the chair of each brother. After allowing the brother a second to catch their breath, she ordered my brother and I to flip over the cards for the dazed pair.

"Yahoo!" yelled one brother.

"Hot damn!" exclaimed the other.

Both had aces.

Mother was flabbergasted because both brothers would now be her new boyfriends.

I went into shock. All of a sudden, my brother and I had two step-daddies at the same time.

Oh my!

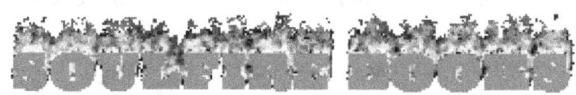

Despite knowing Mother as I did, it was still quite a difficult thing for me to act as if our living arrangements met my approval. I detested the two brothers, but somehow devised a way to co-exist with them, but three weeks into the whole sordid affair, the shit hit the fan at breakfast one Sunday morning.

"Why you so sleepy, lil nigger," the older brother cracked. "Ain't get no sleep last night."

"How somebody gone get some sleep with all the noise y'all be making."

"Noise?" Mother wanted to know, puzzled. "What kind of noises you talking about?"

"The kind y'all be making when y'all be fucking all night. That's what damn noise."

Everything grew silent.

"Anything else you want to know?" I said boldly.

"Why, you lil' nappy-headed, filthy-mouth dog. I should wash yo' dirty mouth out wit' some red devil lye soap."

"Try it, you black bastard, and I'll kill you." I jumped to my feet. "That go for your ass too," I spat at the younger brother. "That's right, I'll kill all both of you motherfuckers."

Too me, it seemed as if I had gone too far too fast, yet I still was not ready to stop, so with a dramatic flair, I popped out my dime store knife. "This heah, a goddamn hawk-bill." I flashed the knife. "This just the motherfucking beginning. Y'all niggers gotta go back home, so forget about me, this nigger heah," I indicated my brother, "and most of all, forget 'bout my Mama."

The backlash was immediate, and that was why I tried to run when I understood just how angry the brothers truly were because some things you just can't expect to forget, good pussy being one of them.

"Don't let them kill me," I hollered at Mother. I didn't know what I was saying......Make them stop.......*Mama!*"

They took me outside. They relished beating me, and they taught me a good lesson. I learned that in a fight, the participant most vulnerable to an ass-whupping is the one who can't fight. Inattention to this most fundamental detail almost got me knocked out.

With my newly-minted ass-whupping, I lie on the ground, calculating the odds of whether I would live or if I would do. I moaned pitifully.

"You'll be a'ight, lil skinny-assed fool."

"One thang you can say 'bout his skinny ass is that he got plenty of heart. He really caught me with a good one a time or two." The younger brother rubbed his jaw, grinning. "Hurt like a son-of-a-bitch."

The older brother sneered. "That lil chump ain't got nutnin'. Ain't gonna have no power in his punch when he gets to be a lil bit older. Probably grow up, hitting like a girl."

"No, I won't neither, you cocksucker," I hollered. "When I grow up and get bug, I'm gonna----."

"Shut the fuck up or I'll stomp a mudhole in yo' half-yellow ass."

"I'll be so glad when you die. You older than dirt, anyhow. Won't nobody come to your funeral. Won't nobody miss, especially my Mama." I got ready to run. "You probably scared to die 'cause you ain't got enough friends to carry your casket. Ain't got nobody 'cept yo' nappy-head baby brother."

Both brothers laughed.

"Tole you the nigger got heart," the younger brother cracked. "Leave him alone."

"You think he tuff," the older brother jeered. "Lil punk ain't shit and I'll prove it. Tell you what, I bet you fifty dollars he can't whup that

21

Taylor boy who stays on the corner by the barbershop. They 'bout the same age."

"Yeah, but the nigger a giant to be his age, He twice the size of this heah scrawny fool. Plus, that Taylor boy a bully."

"Thought you had confidence in yo' boy?"

"I do, but I heard that they already done been fighting that Taylor boy, and they say he pretty damn good."

"I ain't wanting to hear no rap. Is the bet on or what?"

The younger brother eyed me coldly. I had, all of a sudden, become an economic consideration, a pee-wee pawn in a fifty dollar winner-take-all, sibling rivalry bet.

"Yeah, I'll gamble on the skinny motherfucker. Give me ten days to nurse him back to health and to get him ready."

"Ten days?" the older brother scratched his chin. "That's too long. Seven."

"A week?! Fuck it, give me eight and we got us a motherfucking fight."

On a crisp Sunday morning that arrived too damned soon, I became officially anchored to a fifty dollar bet where my adolescence was chained to the very real fact that I could end up getting beat half to death.

Whatever.

To ordinary church folk, I may have looked vaguely foolish, or mad-dog rabid, skipping along behind two grown men, throwing punches at the air.

Fuck the world!

Despite my false start, I was finally on my way to manhood, and too me, on that bright, sunny Sunday, nothing could have been any more exhilarating or inspiring to me than standing on the verge of violence. Violence, I felt, was the portal to my masculinity, and the throes of this discovery made me feel spiritual. Both sides of me, the budding macho as well as the inelegant 'different' were pulled taut, pushed to the absolute limits of what I could become. This fight was not about the mechanics of throwing hands with the Taylor boy. It had everything to do with me battling myself, the two sides of me slugging it out for sole possession of my soul.

22

At any rate, today was the day.

Across the tracks had seen better days. Boarded up storefronts dotted the perimeter on both sides of the dead-end street where a Mom and Pop greasy spoon nestled under a busted neon sign that read: Sugar's.

Halfway around the block was a launderette, and next to the liquor store by the red fire hydrant was a bookstore run by a palm-reading gypsy who sold life insurance on the side. As I moved closer to the blinking yellow light on the adjacent corner, the pent-up lust for blood become a throbbing drumbeat.

A bit farther on, it became impossible for me to prevent the stench of vomit from filling my throat and mouth. I spit out the ugly gob of rising fear despite the fact that it was cathartic, purging me of what I had felt when I had touched my brother in his sleep.

My life flashed before my eyes.

I was aware that my legs felt rubbery, but despite their jello-like consistency, they continued to move forward so I could pursue my interest in becoming free of the restraints of being 'different'. The coming violence would grant me the permission to become normal, whatever that was. Still, I had to risk it.

I was sure I was not the first individual who attempted to conquer a larger-than-life fear via the agency of violence. Moreover, I knew I had to conquer something greater than myself. No, not the Taylor kid. He was an innocent, merely a childish hazard in my path. What I feared most was that if I failed to redeem myself, that I would forever be trapped in the gloom and shadow of not knowing what good pussy was. And that would be devastating to me, someone who had grown up in a home where 'good pussy' was the provision that had satisfied and met all the requirements and needs of everyone in that home. Good pussy and Mother's happy eagerness to use it had made life very, very comfortable for me and my brother.

I had to find some for myself. Someday.

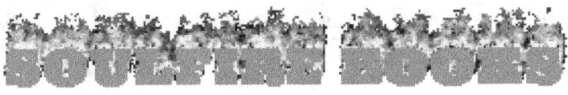

I was tossed into a steel cage. There was a door on each end, and through the other door, a second boy was thrown in. No doubt, the Taylor kid.

Oblivious of everything else, I stared across the cage at him. By mistake, I noticed that he looked ill-treated, and felt a pang of sorrow for him, but this sympathy was swiftly relinquished, replaced by an unbridled manly fury. I would give him no quarter, and I knew that he would repay me in kind. This much I knew to be true.

Throughout the next minute, the effect of being confined in a small enclosure turned stifling, suffocating, and slowly, the two of us were transformed. We both spent the next frantic seconds turning into wild beasts, uncertain of what we were actually capable of doing to the other, but eager for the ritual of transformation to end so we could tear into each other like mad animals.

The cage enraged me.

The cage enraged him.

Finally, one of us noticed that we were too far apart to act out the primitive aggression that boiled our insides. That one person stepped forward. The other, excited by the advance, took additional steps ahead. Neither expected to get there as fast as we did, and the contact was crowned with a tremendous yell from the men who crowded around the cage on all four sides. Their excitement whirled high in the air like electric embroidery that grew more fish-fried with each punch landed.

These men, professional spectators, always on the lookout for blood and gore, had not expected anything so immediately violent. We sold them on youthful mayhem.

He knocked me down.

The trip back to my feet was a difficult journey, and even once I was upright, it was still hard to tell if I was coming or going. But since this was not the first opportunity I had had with being knocked senseless, I did what I had always wanted to do when Mother whacked me.

I swung back. Hard

I hit him with a well-rehearsed uppercut. He hit back. The punch sculpted a temporary dent in my jaw as a tooth became dislodged, lingering forlornly on the edge of my tongue before dropping from my mouth onto the floor of the cage. This overwhelmed me with rage. Of all the teeth in my mouth, my beautiful smile owed its very existence to that one particular molar, and there was no way I could tolerate his handmade travesty upon my person. I swarmed.

He looked somewhat puzzled by the ugliness and abruptness of my renewed attack, but repeated blows to his face clearly explained my intentions. *I was trying to kill his ass!*

As it turned out, the men outside the cage did have some compassion. I guess it was a reminder that slain fighters could generate no revenues, so they----someone----pitched a dingy, yellowing towel in.

Instantly, an official (if he could be called that) rushed in, stopping the melee, but I was too exhausted to celebrate my victory. On top of that, I could hear the younger brother arranging more fights for me. Under this custom, I imagined that I would be too busy fighting to feel, you know, different.

I thought about that, and slowly flashed my now imperfect grin because whatever worked was fine with me. Beating someone up, getting beat up; getting run over by a train; anything was better than feeling like that. You know......different.

Part of his face remained hidden behind a horrible scar, and a hideous sneer criss-crossed that. His eyes were mere dark circles, running round and round in his head, chasing nothing. He was impressive in his deformity.

Different people probably had, at different times, formed different opinions about what had damaged his face. Not me. I, personally, wondered, how, if possible, I could damage him further.

It did not surprise or faze me that I instinctively perceived that he was a winner of many brutal battles. This was simply a realistic observation. Nothing more. Nothing less. In any event, the buck would stop here. He could not win. I wouldn't allow it.

He was fight-wise. He anticipated the bell;, and in one swift motion became one with the sound, propelling himself towards me before the ding was cleared from my ears.

He knocked me down.

He backed off grinning. "I do that all the time," he bragged.

The air smelled sickly sweet as I hopped to my feet. My legs felt sturdy, so I shuffled forward.

He knocked me down again.

The knockdown was legitimate although it seemed that the punch wasn't thrown that hard. Anyway, I had enough sense to hope that he wasn't holding anything back. Struggling to my feet, I saw the fire in his eyes, and I recognized nothing fragile or soft in them, only cold hardness, an unflawed hardness that had no thaw point. His eyes made everything clear. These were the eyes of a killer. However, I would be no ritual sacrifice.

He swung wildly, and I stepped easily out of the blow's path, but it came so close to my nose that I could clearly see the microscopic tears on his tightly-clenched fist. This motherfucker was a killer.

Even though he probably had never personally discerned either the nature or the meaning of fear before, school was definitely in, and I was teaching class. I solidly connected with a three piece combo, two hooks to the head, and a vicious six inch shot to his body. Motherfucker was a damned good student. I popped his head with a rapid succession of right jabs that gave birth to a cement-heavy left hook. Unsurprisingly, he was suddenly gaining insight into the fact that I was not bullshitting, and that I fully intended to fuck him all the way up.

He connected with a return volley of punches of his own, and noting the amount of power he still could muster, I jacked him up, and wrestled him to the ground. Slamming his face into the dirt only added another chapter to the shit he had never experienced until this very moment. When he noticed blood seeping from a gash on his forehead, he seemed to age under the process of acquiring knowledge.

Living organisms are wired internally so that when faced with the distress of getting done in, they are capable of superhuman strength in order to resist, and hopefully to reverse the attempt at murder. Unfortunately, for me, this was one lesson my opponent had learned well. For a brief second, I imagined I was being lifted up in the air by a hydraulic jack. However vivid the imagery, it was wrong. It was not hydraulics that were lifting me, it was his short, powerful arms, and just as soon as I found myself suspended by them in mid-air, he tossed me away as if I were a rotten, black tomato.

I hit the ground, but was not amazed to find that I was not alone. Guess who was there? He leaned over me, his hands and feet conspiring to damage my body. He punched and he kicked. And I didn't consider it much of a fringe benefit that somehow, somewhere he had lost his left shoe since it still hurt like hell when he stomped down on me. I cried out in pain.

The scream was not misleading. I was hurting like a motherfucker. I actively explored prayer.

"Please, God," I begged, "don't let me get murdered."

I got faith, but then out of a dim Sunday school memory, I remember being taught that faith without works is dead, so I went to work. I grabbed that nigger's stomping foot, and twisted it hard to the left until he fell over like a bowling pin. Faith increased. I was up and at his ass. I sprung up like a yellow Jack-In-The-Box and knocked the shit out of him with a punch that just happened to be the one I needed.

Even though the general purpose of the blow was to kill, I was not completely surprised when I discovered him still alive, but squatting on one knee, trying to recover from the punch. I hit him again...BOOM! He was forced to cultivate the dirt floor of the cage as I tried to stomp him into the ground. He hiked his knees up to protect himself while covering himself with his hands.

I stomped.

And stomped.

Despite my vile intentions to kill the boy, I was not that preoccupied with my task that I failed to notice and to admire the perfect symmetry of the little round ball he had rolled up into. Unfortunately, the perfection would avail him nothing. I stomped his black ass harder.

The men outside of the cage were deeply moved by the charm and seduction of savage violence. They whooped and clapped, cramming well-preserved dollar bills through the cage, screaming insanely. "Kill! Kill!"

Legend had it that no one had ever killed anyone inside the cage, so I labored to be the first to send a boy to the Promised Land, but just as soon as I thought that I made death accessible to him, he succeeded in cornering the last bit of his will to live, and struggled to his feet. Apparently, death was no romantic notion to him, and miraculously fought through the haze of seeming defeat, launching a ferocious counterattack. To the accompaniment of his swinging hands and kicking feet, he began to exhort himself to even greater action by chanting some morbid sing-song dirge. I had never heard it before.

"How do you want to die, motherfucker? How do you want to die, motherfucker?" he chanted raggedly. "How do you want to die?"

27

As if I had a preference.

In a valiant effort to cheat death, I used my hands like claws, and pulled at his neck until I had snatched huge chunks of meat from under his chin. He made small, essentially strangled sounds, and when I smashed my knee into his groin, he crumbled like a deflowered virgin.

He doubled over in pain, coughing up specks of blood mingled with fleshy tissue from his mangled throat. While bent over, I slammed a tremendous sledgehammer fist into the small of his back. His knees buckled.

And hen contrary to everything that could have happen or should have happened, my violent assault was ended as he moaned like some wounded beast, and shoved his head upwards. The back of his skull crashed into the front of my face. Intense pain rumbled through my mouth, and a tooth tumbled out. Blood gushed from my nose. Stars danced before my eyes, and there was a humming in my ears that seemed unnecessarily loud. I was dazed, but aware enough to know that I still had to protect myself.

Whimpering softly, I back-pedaled, seeking shelter from the bloodlust that glowed in my opponent's eyes. This time when he came at me, there was a renewed value to the attack. He wasn't just advancing forward to button-up my lip, or to blacken my eye because my apparent weakness had granted him license to go way beyond that.

He moved in for the kill.

His tightly clenched fists thudded and thundered upside my head. They were a curse to my consciousness, a scourge to my bodily welfare. There was enough brutality to put me to sleep, and when he slammed a hard jab on my ear, he seemed bitterly amused. I imagine that it was then that he realized that the punch was a good start to ending the fight, so he did what came naturally to him. He hit me again. This time, harder.

I was, by now, barely sane, consciousness having long ago fled. Nothing propped me up on my trembling legs but insanity, and dutifully I cursed it.

He drove me back into the cage, and pummeled my body until I wanted to vomit,

"Fall." He ordered. "Fall!"

I heard his voice. It was dismal-sounding, and coming from what seemed to be a long distance.

"Fall!"

His voice was raw, without culture or humanity. Mean. Ugly.

"Fall!"
Four punches later, he said it once more.
"Fall!"
I did.

C H A P T E R 4

Mother was restless.

Some three blocks beyond our house, there was a rickety old store where Mother went a lot. The interior of the store, and none of the good sold therein interested her in the least; however, the man who owned the store did.

Mother said the man and her were culturally compatible. They both were light-skinned. In the past, she had failed to show any concern or attention to "red" niggers who she put down as traditional 'pretty boys' who aren't shit in bed.

The store man, she found somewhat exotic. Whenever the two brothers were out of earshot, she was always gushing to either my brother or I about how sexy he was with his luxurious hair and bow legs.

In a nostalgic return to her former ways, Mother decided that she was ready to entertain other men. She was still willing to retain the brothers as select members of her bedroom, but as she tried to explain it, she had gotten a signal---from somewhere---informing her to graciously share herself with more than just a pair of men.

"What?!" the younger brother shrieked while listening to Mother's explanation.

The older brother was equally confused.

"What?!"

"It's sorta hard to explain," Mother confessed, "but it's kinda like a light comes on inside my pussy, and this light, you know, is like a signal for me to, well------."

"Give away mo' pussy," one of the brothers interrupted.

Mother sneered. "You make it sound like so....so disgusting."

"And just what do you think it is, woman?" It was the younger of the two. "You givin' 'way something that you ain't supposed to be giving away. Yo' pussy is the bond that keeps this lil union of ours together, and I seriously don't think me and my brother need no help with it."

"But It's mine."

"Naw, ho, it ain't neither," the elder brother spoke. "I hate to bust yo' bubble, but yo' pussy ain't yours."

Mother frowned. "Whose is it, then? The last time I looked, the motherfucker was still between my legs, just as big and fat and juicy as always." Mother deepened her frown. "And just who the hell you supposed to be, telling me that I don't own my own pussy. All bitches got 'em, and this red one," she pointed at her crotch, "all mine." Mother put her hands on her hips, defiant. "This pussy mine."

"It's like this," the older brother remarked wearily. "Just 'cause it's between yo' legs don't mean that's it's yours."

"And why not?"

"Dammit, bitch, when you got a man---."

"Or two," quickly added the baby boy.

The oldest brother nodded at his younger sibling and continued talking. "If you just got to know, bitch, you a sharecropper, dig? You might've growed it, but you can't sell it, and you damn sho' can't give it away."

"And why is that?"

"Cause it belong to the master."

Mother burst into derisive laughter. "So, y'all the masters of my pussy?"

The younger brother shrugged, in full agreement with his brother's assessment. "We don't make the rules, ho."

"And I can't give it away without y'all say-so?"

"Like I done already said, ho, we don't make no motherfucking rules" The younger brother snickered. "We just benefit from 'em."

Mother was incensed. "Well, let me have my say 'bout this bullshit both of y'all talking. You gonna have to find some other stupid, country-assed girl to tell that sharecropper shit to. This pussy mine. I

31

done grew it, and now that it's ripe and ready, I'm fucking who I damn well please. Furthermore, if I take a notion to give that pretty, red nigger down at the store some ass, ain't nuthin' neither of y'all can do to stop it."

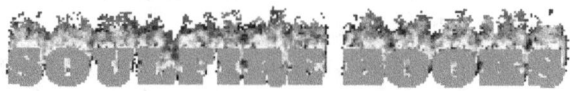

The pretty, red-assed nigger down at the store was buried on Thursday. Mother made us attend. She looked solemn and beautiful, but she also knew the brothers meant business.

We sat on the left side of the church, and I felt stiff and sissified in my blue suit which didn't fit all that well. I would need a good fight after this was all over with. Thank heavens, I could always depend on violence to purge me of my feelings of inadequacy which kept popping up with more and more frequency. It was disturbing.

Anyway, Mother was sobbing loudly when they came in. She stopped instantly. The brothers sat down next to her.

"What nerve you bastards got," she whispered, "showing up in here of all places."

"Hell, a funeral is just as good a place to go to as anywhere else."

The younger brother leaned over. "Ain't you something else? You the same one who always be telling us to find somewhere to go where there ain't no booze or floozies." He looked around. "Well, bitch, this is it."

"Keep your voice down," Mother hissed. "You know what I meant, you damn fool. Even if you didn't, I know you know the difference between finding somewhere to go, and giving us some place to go."

"What up talking 'bout, bitch?"

"You know good and damn well what I'm talking about, nappy-headed nigger."

"Well, I sho' as hell don't," the eldest replied. "Don't know and don't wanna know."

"Don't start that shit like you dumb. Y'all bastards the ones that killed that red nigger up yonder in that casket just as sho' as my pussy good."

"Shut up, hussy. I don't got no time to be arguing wit' yo' no good, red ass up in heah at this solemn occasion."

32

"Y'all killer Joes ain't worth shit," Mother hissed. "Killer Joe", she hissed at one brother. "Killer Joe," she hissed at the other.

One of them slapped Mother. The other clamped a hand over her mouth so she couldn't scream, and they dragged her out of the church, kicking and wiggling.

The preacher preached. "Sometimes, we all wish that death would get lost, take a wrong turn, or run down a dead-end street, but he don't. That ol' Grim Reaper knows his way around." The preacher shook his head sadly. "Just two doors down from this good, law-abiding, church-going businessman, lying here, cold and dead, in this lonely box lived a lost soul, hell-bent for a good killing, and he got passed over. Death knew who he wanted. Granted, it was a bad choice, but that's how it goes when ignorant folks want to send a man's life on a long vacation, but trust me, whoever did this dirty deed to our beloved brother will catch fire in hell."

With a bit of help from the people at the funeral home, the brothers were actually prevented from killing Mother. She appeared frazzled, but apparently pleased with the rescue attempt. Other than a near-perfect black eye, she retained a big dose of her usual sexiness.

We were ushered to the gravesite, and whatever it was that Mother may have felt she had lost to the grave was left there. In an abrupt huff, she shuffled me and my brother away from the hole in the ground.

"Let's go," she said, "this nigger's done for." On the drive home, Mother flirted with the colossal idea of leaving the brothers. "We got to rid of them niggers," she said. "They ain't shit."

To me, though, the biggest surprise was not the discovery that good pussy was worth killing and dying for, but rather that the die-hard connoisseurs of good pussy considered it a sacrilege to let it get away from them. According to masculine lore, 'if good pussy, once obtained, ever got away from you, your brain would shrivel up and it would drive you crazy'.

As soon as we got home, the brothers confronted Mother.

"Ho, you under house arrest."

"And you better act like you like it."

"Okay, babies," Mother sighed, "if that's the way y'all want it. I'm sorry. I've been a bad girl", she purred, "but before y'all punish me, I get to make one final request, don't I?"

"Last request? Ho, we ain't fixing to execute yo' ass. Bitch, we just fixing to teach you a lesson."

33

"Honey, I don't care about being punished 'cause I wants to be a good girl, and I think I'm capable of being everything you want me to be, and if you think punishment is the answer, then I won't say shit. But, first, let me cook you a good cat-fish dinner with a mess of collard greens." She smiled. "How that sound?"

"Stupid."

"Stupid?"

"Hell yeah, bitch, you ain't poisoning us."

I couldn't help but laugh.

During the period of Mother's house arrest, I began fighting more, and with startling precision I demolished all my opponents, beating two of them to senseless pulps. I was good. To win, I employed no special techniques, but chief among my skills was my unrestrained fury. I fought to heal the scars of my soul. Also unique was the fact that I had no fear of punishment. This made me feel invincible. Nobody could whup me.

It wasn't something that I was philosophical about because being as tough as nails was simply a part of my personal history that protected me emotionally, that is, until those old feelings would surface from deep inside the recesses of my being. Then, I would want to destroy myself.

What seemed to be emerging from this inner turmoil was nothing complex or brilliant. What basically appeared was an image of myself as a symbol of something else, knowing somehow that the consequences of being transformed would shatter my illusions and force me to lie down with my delusions.

It was what it was, but for once, it felt as if I was going deliberately slow as fast as I possibly could.

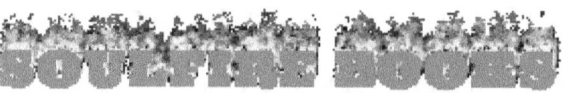

It was no accident. As it happened, the fire started shortly after Mother had me and my brother safely in the big Buick. She drove bat-out-of-hell fast for a few blocks, and then came to an almost complete stop as if she was contemplating the merits of breaking another law so immediately after committing the first. She adjusted the pace of the car until it was under the speed limit, and then turned completely around, heading back in the direction from which we had come, back towards the burning house.

She stopped about fifty yards away, and silently observed the damage done. After a few seconds of watching, she slowly fanned her perfumed, gloved hand slowly across her brooding, beautiful face. This was the goodbye wave.

Farewell.

My brother nudged me roughly in the side with his bony elbow, his wide eyes were question marks. We both clearly knew who had set the house on fire. Now, we simply desired to know what had happened to the brothers. What had prevented them from waking up? Why wouldn't they have run out of the burning house, screaming and cursing at Mother. *What had Mother done?*

A great deal of the black, night sky was finger-painted with the red, yellow, and blue haze of the fire that was so brilliant in the darkness that it looked like the urban edition of Armageddon. Suddenly, the delicately-shingled roof exploded with an agonizing groan, was silent for a brief moment, and then crashed inward with a robust roar.

My brother sighed deeply. I merely settled down into my seat cushion knowing that we had just crossed the frontier of another one of Mother's adventures. Neither my brother nor I were fazed. Death and destruction had always been the trademarked symbols of Mother's declaration of independence.

Wherever this new town was where Mother was now compelling us to call home had seen better days. Now, it was not much more than the ultimate expression of gloom, but that would soon change. Mother's presence would demand it.

"I'm so fine," Mother confided to us shortly after our arrival, "that I'm gonna roast these niggers' guts."

Apparently sickened by the fact that the first male she encountered did not cheerfully submit to her sexy, intoxicating presence, she huffed out of the general store, and drove off. Around a deserted corner, she halted the car, and dashed to the trunk. She fussed and

35

fumed, rummaging through her clothes until she located the dress she wanted. It was red. And tight-fitting. She changed into it right on the spot.

My brother closed his eyes.

I giggled. She patted her ass at me.

"In time, you'll know," she said. After re-arranging her hair, re-applying a fresh coat of a redder lipstick, and tightening the belt that encircled her waist, she brimmed with renewed confidence. "Only women as beautiful as myself get a second chance to make a first impression," she lectured my brother and me. Then, she returned to the country store.

The man's neck twisted grotesquely as he strained to get a better look at Mother. She wasted no time in ignoring him, and she made his head swivel dangerously on his neck as she sashayed purposely slow behind a rack of Campbell's soup. When she disappeared from his view, the customer at the counter instantly became a distraction.

"Could you please hurry," the owner of the store barked rudely as his eyes fell longingly at the spot where Mother had last been seen. He faked a cough of impatience. "You know something," he explained to the man at the cash register, "today I'm going to make you a lucky winner."

"Of what?"

"Of being such a loyal customer."

The man brightened. "Well, what do I win?"

"Anything you want, just as long as you can get it and get the hell out of here in fifteen seconds."

The man snatched up two country hams, a dozen eggs, and a Jet magazine before dashing out of the front door. Left with no other distractions, the store owner approached the soup rack, circling from the rear, his sizable interest growing even more sizable. He took another long look at Mother's backsides and coughed.

"Ahem."

Mother paid him no attention.

"Excuse me, Miss," he asked, "but weren't you here just a little while ago?"

"No," Mother lied, "evidently, you have me confused with my sister, but I don't see how that could be possible. She's-she's so plain." Mother smiled.

The man gasped audibly. "Anything I can do for you would be a pleasure."

"I know," Mother purred.

The man looked Mother over boldly. "In that case, you may have just stumbled upon the first black genie known to exist." He flexed his muscles. "Feel free to test my powers," he grinned.

"Where's a good hotel?"

A frown creased the man's face. "You underestimate my ability as a genie, my friend. There is no genie that I ever heard of that would allow a beautiful princess to occupy a hotel."

"Is that so?"

"Yes, especially when he owns the finest house in town."

"Oh?" Mother's eyes widened. She became inquisitive. "In addition to being a genie, what are you......Mayor?"

"Even better. I'm the preacher."

"Preacher?" Mother moved closed, running her tongue suggestively across her brightly-colored lips, "but what will your congregation say?"

The preacher chuckled. "Let them talk. And let us go home."

I had digested the defeat well. I found that it was less a comment about my life than I had imagined it would have been, but still I did not particularly enjoy losing. It was a personal chronicle I could live without.

Abruptly, I had forgotten, or had chosen to forget exactly how long it had truly been since my terrible beating, and though I no longer harbored any physical scars, the echoes of that moment haunted me, leaving me with a bitter mix of revenge and regret.

Sometimes, in the still wee hours of the morning when the youthful exuberance of dawn was so full of itself, I would be thrown back headlong into that inhumane moment, and no matter how removed I tried to be from that ugly day, the complete thoroughness of the way in which he had destroyed me never lost its reputation to frighten me.

From time to time, I feuded with every emotion I had ever developed, and despite the enormous humiliation, it was with a gratitude far deeper, and more significant, than anything I'd previously known. It caused me to rejoice. Those odd feelings were gone.

Hallelujah!

Sadly, there were not gone for good. Or long.

The month of April had brought the boy from only-the-devil-knows-where, but when he got to where I was, he flipped my world upside down. He was a mere wisp of a human male, a size not many black boys came in. Paper-thin. Delicate. His only strength being his intense darkness. His person crackled and bristled with an eerie strangeness that stamped an aura of the taboo about him, and when he walked out of the Preacher's store that evening, it was with a high-spirited gait that said 'come-and-get-me.

"Who the fuck is that?" I blurted.

"Watch your mouth, young man."

I apologized, "Okay, okay, Preacher-man, but who is that nigger?" I frowned, realizing how much that sounded like something Mother would say. "He-he looks real cool", I lied, trying to hide my sudden interest.

"Well, he ain't," the Preacher rasped.

"Ain't what?"

"Cool."

"Why?"

"Because he's as hot in the tail as----"

"My Mama," I finished innocently.

"Boy, you just mind your own business, and stay away from that abominable child of the devil. He's a sinner."

"But ain't that a sin what you be doing with my Mama?"

"And what do you know about sinning?"

"Probably nothing," I admitted, "but I know about lying, and I know that's what you be telling folks when you say my Mama is your cousin from Texas."

The preacher was getting angry. "And how do you know we're not cousins, your Mama and me?"

I was quiet.

"See there, Mr. Smarty-Pants, you don't know if it's a lie or not, so I think you owe me an apology."

"No, I don't neither."

"You don't. Why?"

"We're not from Texas!"

I dashed out of the store. Outside, the sun was a fragile ball of warmth, dispersing heat, and then hiding behind big, fluffy clouds. Thus anchored on the underside of the sky, the sun made piles of simmering shadows that grew out of everything in sight.

I jumped over the prickly shadow of a rose bush, and ran through a chilly haze of transparent greyness that belonged to the Volunteer Fire Department building, but as I prepared to spin around the body of a dead rat, the boy popped out of nowhere, a mixture of fire and ice.

His breath blew over me as he spoke. "Whatcha doing, stranger?"

"Nuthin'." I sounded bashful.

"Do you like playing by yourself?"

Growing defensive, I snapped. "I wasn't playing. I'm not a baby."

"Looked like playing too me."

"I'm a fighter, and fighters don't play."

"A fighter," he giggled girlishly. "Fighters have big muscles, don't they?"

I angrily rolled up the sleeves of my shirt. "See."

He touched my arm. I grew dizzy.

Satisfied?" I let me arm go limp. "Tole' you I was a fighter." My eyes quizzed him.

"I'm a lover," he finally confessed.

"What do you love," I teased, "snakes, snails, and puppy dog tails?"

"Thought you said that you wasn't a baby."

"I ain't."

"Well, that was childish."

I apologized, not wishing to anger him.

"Don't play with love," he scolded me. "Love is serious."

"So what, nigger," I shot back, "I'm a fighter; tough. Don't need no motherfucking love."

"You lie. The whole world needs love."

"Not me."

"You do, too."

"I don't neither."

He quickly pressed his lips to the side of my face. "You need love." Then he ran away.

I tried to yell out to him to come back, but I couldn't do anything but feel hot all over.

"Bitch!" the preacher cursed, "even though you're the most extraordinary women I've ever been in bed with, I don't know how to handle this shit you talking about us just being friends. I would rather for a jack-leg preacher from somewhere across town to stand over my closed casket, preaching my eulogy that have you to walk away from me."

"It worked! It worked!" Mother clapped her together merrily. "It worked."

The preacher was totally confused. Mother kissed his cheek. "I was just fooling around. I just wanted to make you mad, so when you get to church, you can preach up a storm. You been needing a lil bit more fire in your sermons, honey. I was only trying to help. Ain't I something?"

"Bitch, you about to get fucked up playing silly games with me. I don't like to be fooled with when it comes to----."

"Good pussy. I know," said Mother, "but I was just being a naughty girl. Don't be mad," she pleaded. "Nigger, I ain't ever leaving you 'cause ain't nothing like a low-down, sneaky-assed, pussy-starved reverend. Now, you just get your fine ass on down to that church, preach real pretty, and then come on back home to Big Mama. I'm gonna have a big surprise for you."

Time flew.

No sooner had the preacher tucked in his sermon with the final Amen than he was off the pulpit, and out of the church's door. He headed home. For the present moment, his greatest ambition was to get home and to put 'a fucking on that red ho that she would not soon forget'. His car went fast. At the speed he was going, everything appeared strikingly similar, but he paid little attention. He simply concentrated on pushing his automobile through the blur even quicker.

As he zoomed past the town's tall, slanted water tower, he made up two brand new sexual positions that he fully intended to try out today on that red bitch. After this afternoon, she would not just admire his bedroom skills. No sir, that hussy would stand in awe of his performance.

He slammed into the front yard, parking his Caddy next to Mother's Buick as if they were metal playmates before bursting through the front door, flinging his robe to the floor. He screamed loudly.

"Today, I shall increase your knowledge. Bitch!"

The house was quiet. The preacher divested himself of his remaining garments, and crept to his bedroom door. His hand reached for the knob. Stopped.

What?

40

The preacher couldn't believe his ears.

Moans. And he knew them well. Someone was in there------in his bed, fucking his woman! He couldn't believe it. His first thought was to steal a glance through the keyhole, but spying seemed so undignified. Shit, he would kick in the door. It was his house, his bed; his bitch.

He raised his foot.

"Oh baby," Mother moaned loudly. "Damn, it's so big and so long and so damn good.'

The preacher's foot dropped.

"Why me?" Mother screamed out in ecstasy. "Why me? Of all the bitches in the world, why did you choose me to fuck so good on this wonderful Sunday morning. Since when did I get so lucky. I love you, nigger."

The preacher's face contorted in rage. "Bitch, you no-good slut."

"Go away," Mother screamed back. "I'm busy. Go turn water into wine or something. Raise the dead; anything. Just leave me alone so I can make this sweet nigger cum."

Clutching his chest, the preacher gasped loudly, his eyes paled inside their sockets, turning milkshake white. "Oh my Jesus," he groaned, "my heart." He stumbled away from the bedroom door, and ambled in the direction of the bathroom. "Oh shit, where's my pills?"

Mother had them, and after a few seconds, I knocked on the bedroom door. "It's safe, Ma, He ain't moving no more."

Mother emerged from the empty bedroom, fully dressed, with every hair on her head strictly in place. She stared at the preacher and winked her eye at me and my brother. "It worked!" she gushed. "Sometimes, what a nigger thinks is worse than what he knows. Always remember that." Then she threw back her head and laughed wildly. "Ain't no man in the world that can make me moan like that."

She   had   a   good   laugh.

CHAPTER 5

Equally troubling to the local church-goers was not only the fact that Mother had immediately started selling wine and beer out of the general store, but that she had opened up a gambling room in the back.

"It's a den of iniquity," the church ladies protested.

"She sells strong drink," others remarked.

Mother was unfazed. "This joint is mine, and if I take a notion to sell ass at a discount, then that is what I will do. It's like the lawyer said, the will didn't stipulate what I could or couldn't do with the store. Hmmph, I could sell bottled piss if I want to. These old biddies better not start messing with the queen."

But the old biddies did.

Only seven people were in the back of the store gambling when 'the old biddies' arrived. They entered the store, snarling and chanting. Immediately, they attacked the wine counter, and gleefully began smashing the bottles.

I dutifully ran to the back to get Mother. "Mama, Mama," I hollered. "it's some old hoes in the store busting up all the liquor."

Mother tore into them without hesitation, pushing, shoving, and slapping their powdered faces. "Stop it," she commanded, "or I'll tear your old-assed arms off your old-assed bodies. What the fuck done got into y'all senile bitches anyhow?"

"We're against wine and beer." One chanted.

"We're against gambling," another added.

"We're against sin," a third one shouted.

"So we're all against you," they all chorused.

"And I'm against broke, discouraged, near-death, old busy-bodies." Mother looked at the women. "Pay for the damages and please leave."

"We are not here to pay you. We're here to run you out of town."

Mother turned businesslike. "One hundred dollars will be sufficient to cover the damages." She held out her hand. "You the bitch doing all the yapping, so I assume you the one that's gonna be paying. No checks, please. You can't pass them at church so I don't want 'em here." She stared at the woman. "Gimme my money, ho."

At her core, the lead biddie was a mostly non-violent woman, but, for some reason, Mother brought out the worst in her. Maybe the fumes from the spilled wine had screwed up her senses and had somehow wrecked her sense of judgment. In any event, she slapped at Mother.

Being the seasoned street-fighter that she was, Mother saw the blow coming. She moved so quick, it was almost as if she had anticipated the assault even before it had developed in the old woman's mind. Mother executed a crude bob-and-weave. A red patent leather handbag smashed atop her skull. The lick froze Mother into her crouch. A blue handbag whistled through the air, landing with a dull thud just above Mother's left ear. After that, a dizzying array of purses stormed upside Mother's head until she was forced to retreat.

Breathing hard, Mother kicked off her heels. "Y'all bitches don't know what trouble y'all black asses gonna be in when I catch my breath."

And then it happened.

The youngest of the old biddies, the quaintly well-preserved one with plum-colored highlights in her grey hair, charged. She lunged towards Mother in a heated rush, and skidded to within inches of Mother's nose.

Mother introduced her to a stiff sock on the jaw. Thoroughly shaken, the woman backed up a few paces, lowered her head like a battering ram and charged again, huffing and puffing hard. She and Mother tangled, falling back onto the counter, knocking over a bubble-gum machine, and a display for Lucky Strike cigarettes.

The other biddies studied the fight like ancient battle generals, falling under the spell of combat, up close and personal, but when Mother

43

hammered their comrade's head with a can of pork and beans, they dived in on Mother like a troop of vultures. Their mission was not be imperiled.

My brother and I joined the fray on the side of our Mother, but before we knew it, the place was swarming with the police. They called for the paddy wagon.

They came again on Sunday.

This time when the old biddies came, they brought with them a delegation of pretty, young girls, wide-eyed and excited in their Sunday dresses and their flashy hair ribbons. They entered the store like a platoon of little sun-burnt Shirley Temple dolls, but quickly broke rank when they saw the well-stocked candy counter.

"Help yourselves," Mother commanded the girls in her most charitable voice.

"Hold it!" the lead biddie cackled, halting the girls in their tracks "we are not here on a candy-hunting expedition. We are here so you can see what the face of sin looks like, and once you recognize it, to either stand and fight it with the sword of righteousness, or run like a dog as far away from it as you can get."

"And she," the youngest biddie sneered, "is evil in the flesh."

"But her dress is so pretty," one girl exclaimed.

"And her hair."

"Just look at her shoes."

"*Shut up!*" It was the lead bidddie. She was mad. "Listen to me good." She pointed a bony, accusing finger at Mother. "That's what sin is----pretty. You think people would be attracted to it if it was ugly and nasty-looking. Listen well, my children. If sin looked like death-on-the-corner, do you think men would flock like chickens around it?"

"No ma'am" the girls said in unison.

"Well, then," Mother hissed, you done made your point. Leave now, please." She smiled sweetly at the girls. "The candy is still free."

The lead biddie held her ground. "Someone has to have the courage, the, the....what's the word I'm looking for?'

"Try <u>stupid</u>, bitch," Mother interjected.

The little girls giggled.

"Oh, it's funny, is it?" The lead biddie shook her head. "Those who laugh at sin are the minimum wage-workers of the devil, and every time they giggle, they get a raise until they get so rich in sin that they laugh all the way to the hellfire." She took a deep breath, but swooned when the town's doctor entered. "You, too, doc? It was by your hands that most of these darlings were born, and now you, of all folks, come her to try your hand at poker, tonk, pitty-pat, and Lord-knows-what-else." She grasped both her hands and thrust them towards heaven. "Even skilled hands, when idle, reaches for the devil's pleasure."

Mother sneered. "If you old hoes were somewhere in somebody's bed fucking and making young'uns, then his skilled hands would stay busy at his doctoring, so blame your own old asses."

"Come out of her, Satan," the heavyset biddie yelped. "Come out right now and leave her alone." She looked around helplessly, sweat popping out on her brow. "Since we don't have a flock of swine for you to go into, I beseech thee, Satan, to enter into that pound of pork chops, and cast yourself into the sea." She grabbed the meat, but Mother wrestled it from her.

"Bitch," Mother scolded. "That damn pig is fresh. Don't you know better than to be fucking with folks' food. Pork and pussy, two thangs a nigger will kill for."

"Cover your ears, little innocent ones."

"They ain't heard shit yet," Mother warned. "And if you don't get them out of here, I'm gonna show them my pussy, and teach them how I make it sang."

Hearing that the old biddies rushed the young girls out of the store.

Mother prayed.

The nucleus of every sad moment I had faced since the day I had played in the shadows down by the Fire Department was directly related to him.

Following these tense moments, I brooded deeply, pondering the possible whereabouts of the wafer-thin boy. How could he continue to draw shelter from life after causing me to die inside--- slowly, membrane by membrane; piece by piece?

Where was he?

A little while later, I was forced to stop brooding long enough to try to figure out what had gotten into Mother. *She got married!*

I refused to understand at first.

"I don't love the bastard," Mother explained. "I love y'all."

"But you marrying him," I said accusingly, "and you ain't even known him but nine days."

"Don't fret, nigger. Your Mama knows exactly what she's doing, and believe you me, he's gonna wish he had known what he was in for when he asked me to marry him."

The dazed look on my face was not accidental. I sincerely didn't get it.

"For women such as myself, marriage is a resource, especially when it comes to men like that."

I nudged my brother, but he wouldn't ask, so I had to do it. "And just what kind of man is he?"

"Rich," Mother chirped brightly. "Richer than a motherfucker."

"Oh."

"*Oh!?* Is oh all you can say, you little ungrateful bastard. Just as soon as I say I Do, y'all niggers gonna be shitting in high cotton." She laughed. "That sucker don't know the exchange rate of putting his name on good pussy, and both y'all better watch and learn so some trifling hussy won't do y'all like I'm fixing to do this nigger." She flashed a dark, sinister smile. "Sometimes, a man's money ain't nothing but a monument to what lies between a fine bitch's legs."

Mother then patted her hair, put on her veil, and sashayed out of the dressing room. My brother and I scurried out into the wedding chapel. The wedding hall was big and empty. The figures in the huge, stained-glassed windows shone like red and green gems, lighting up the whole insides of the chapel. This dazzling iridescence was partnered with the shimmering translucent beauty of the white, hot light cast off by the golden chandeliers that dangled from the ceiling.

The unoccupied pews were cloaked in the dark radiance of a glossy spectacular brown while beneath them rested a wonderfully ornate carpet of red and green with golden flecks woven in and out of the plush crevices of the pile.

Hired hands lit the long, tapered, elegant white candles that graced the altar next to where the Justice of The Peace stood, waiting; looking solemn. He fidgeted, and this ever so slight movement

46

manufactured music. It rose softly, but steadily from somewhere hidden, and as soon as I recognized the distinctive tune, I gazed up to see some stranger, another hired hand, escorting Mother down the aisle.

I glanced at my brother whose eyes glistened with tears. He was overwhelmed by the pageantry of it all. I leaned over and hushed-mouth whispered in his ear. "This ain't real, remember. Mama is just bullshitting."

He quickly wiped his eyes. Now, excitement filled them. This was entertainment, another one of Mother's sideshows; a circus where we always laughed loudest, longest, and last. Whatever the circumstances, Mother knew best.

At the last minute, the Justice of The Peace smelled a rat, sniffing out the charade, and wanted nothing more to do with this farce than was covered by his fee. He rushed through the ceremony, the couple exchanged vows, kissed, and it was over. We left.

Back at home, Mother changed clothes and sang a happy song. She kissed us goodbye.

"Mama?" I said

Mother stopped in her tracks. She froze. "What?"

"Our new name. What is it?"

"Don't even worry 'bout no new fucking name. This will be all over before your old name gets cold. Bye-Bye."

As soon as she was gone, visions of the wafer-thin boy danced through my head as my life assumed a tempo that slowed almost to a halt. I had to see that nigger, to view him in all his youth magnificence, and to harmlessly gamble with the notion that he could make me whole. In many ways, it seemed as though I would never be free from the desire I selfishly cultivated of wanting to sandwich him between everything I did from dawn to dark for each and every day that I existed.

Oh what pain!

Despite the danger of totally destroying the fabric of my life by hoping, wishing, and waiting to be close to him always, I had to constantly confide to myself that I no longer cared. It had to be him-----or no one at all.

On a Wednesday night that rained, I began my trek. I set out to find him, the object of my desire. The gloomy weather well matched my attitude, and as I rounded the first corner on the first street of my quest, I momentarily wanted to turn back. Something cautioned me not to

47

proceed any farther, not to take another step into this blistering unknown. I forced myself onward. "Go!" I commanded myself.

Thus committed, I became an apprentice to whatever difficulty the night and the gloom produced. At my first stop, I was greeted with curses; the mean, evil words rusting away in the wind, but never losing their angry sting. Walking stiffly, I forged ahead, a plaything of the elements. After a few blocks, my attitude actually improved. Clearly, I would not die tonight. Disappointed, hell yes. Dead, not hardly. Still, my resolve to find him became even more ferocious.

I knocked on another door.

"Why are you out here on such a night as this," an old lady asked me, "and where you are going?"

After three more knocks on three more doors, I sought, whenever possible, to question my sanity, but oddly enough, I always managed to assure myself that I was of sound mind.

Another knock. Another door.

"I'm looking for someone."

"In heavens' name who, and what made you think you might find that someone here?"

"i-I"

"I live alone. Goodbye, young man."

One of the final stops I made on that side of the street was a blue wood house with a weather vane on the roof. Attached to the heavy oak door was a brass knocker. I slammed it against the wooden door. Thrice.

"Yes?'

"I'm sorry to bother you but---."

"You're hungry, aren't you?"

"No ma'am."

"Oh my goodness," the matronly woman exclaimed, "you're lost."

I shook my head, and dislodged drops of rain fell on her hand.

"Don't tell me that you have run away from home?" She smiled, "I commend your choice of nights," she whispered behind her hand like a spy in an old black and white movie. "Please come in."

Within minutes, I was dry and wrapped in a warm, fluffy towel, sitting in front of a fireplace, shivering yet content.

"I don't know where you thought you were headed, but quite by good luck, you have chosen the proper path to a cup of hot chocolate."

The cup of steaming hot chocolate was pleasingly delightful, and during the first half of my visit, I learned that she was the only surviving triplet of the only triplets ever born in the county. They had all been Sunday school teachers, and had an insatiable craving to be good Samaritans, black agents of mercy.

The second hour found her fondly discussing her husband who secretly had wanted to be a pirate, but came no closer to his goal than serving a stint on a trawler, scrimping for shrimp.

As for her children, the two girls had done rather nicely for themselves. The sons, well, the oldest was an insurance salesman. As for the other three, I don't remember what happened to any of them. I fell asleep.

My first choice was to believe I had been dreaming, but I was not. Someone was forcefully shaking me awake. I threw open my tired eyes.

"What are you doing here?"

Wakefulness developed swiftly out of the vague nothingness where sleep had cast me, and upon closer scrutiny, I perceived, quite fondly, that this was no deception. My heart danced.

"I asked you a question. What are you doing here?"

I smiled lazily, looking up at the wafer-thin boy. "Where did you come from?"

The light that seemed to dart from his eyes resulted in my experiencing violent, internal convulsions that scrambled my brain. When he leaned over me, hovering only inches from my face, his nubile body emitted a warmth that no fire could equal.

"I'm the one asking the questions. Now, answer me. What are you doing here? Asleep."

First came the loss of my voice, followed by a deafness in my ears that cloaked his voice with a musical otherworldliness.

"Do you want your face slapped?"

"No," I croaked, "please don't do that."

"Then give me some answers," he demanded.

"I-I was, er, came looking for you."

"How did you know I lived here?"

"I didn't know."

"Mighty funny, here you are."

I sighed heavily. "I know."

"Are you what the cat dragged in?" he said playfully.

"Do you want to know the truth?"

"Of course."

"I knocked on every door in town until I found you."

"You lie."

I smiled. "Almost. I did come out tonight looking for you, and I didn't know you lived here. I never asked."

"The lady----."

"My grandmother."

"Was so nice that I just wanted to listen to her all night and-----."

"You had given up, hadn't you?"

"No. Never," I responded truthfully.

"Good," he exclaimed joyfully. "Let's talk."

The local townspeople will forever tend to dwell upon the fact that Mother even got married, but what amazed me was how quickly the marriage ended. Almost overnight, Mother had introduced a brand new controversy into a town that had never grown to appreciate trouble as an ornament.

After the honeymoon, Mother flew into town in a wild rage.

"The only thing anyone can do for me," she huffed, "is to show me the office of a good attorney. I want a divorce, quick, fast, and in a damn hurry. Ain't no way in hell, I'm gonna stay married to a motherfucker with an itty-bitty dick. That's asking too damned much."

So great was her rage that when her husband sent his lawyer to speak with her in a bid for reconciliation, she drew a pistol on him, and then threw him out of the house.

"Tell him we'll talk when his dick grows up," Mother spat.

Despite all her negative bluster, an itty-bitty dick did have some merit, and in this case, its worth was half of everything the "silly nigger' owned. Even Mother called it a real treasure......in more ways than one.

Would Mother's latest gambit pay off?

To be certain, the accusation of a tiny dick lashed out at the very fabric of a man's sexual survival, and the very idea of having the bad news broadcast in public would be enough to cower most men, but not the silly nigger. He fought fire with fire.

"And just what the fucking hell is this?" Mother screamed at the lawyer.

The silly nigger's lawyer spoke up. "My client called it Donkey Kong."

"*Donkey Kong*?! Mother repeated, incensed. She turned to her lawyer. "And just what in the fucking hell is a Donkey Kong?"

"From what his attorney would have us to believe, it is a plaster cast of his client's sexual organ."

Mother stared at it blankly. "His, and who else's. That silly nigger wishes he had a dick like that." She gazed at it lovingly. "I wish he had a dick like that because if he did, I'd have his ass in bed somewhere making his toenails sweat."

"Well," Mother's attorney expounded, "your husband claims that the replica is correct in both length and width."

"Excuse me," the silly nigger's lawyer said, "but I was made to understand by my client that the representation is not totally accurate as to the actual length and girth."

"I'll say," Mother sighed.

"Actually," the silly nigger's lawyer continued, "it's off by a few inches."

"Longer?' Mother's lawyer inquired hopefully.

"No. Shorter."

Mother was mad, truly angry.

"It is the sincere contention of my client that his, er, dick for lack of a better word, wouldn't get completely erect because the female who poured the original cast was ugly."

"Well, I never," Mother moaned.

"And that's only half the equation," the lawyer insisted. "There's more."

"Such as?" Mother's lawyer countered.

"Women who would be quite willing to testify and to confirm the status of that replica." The silly nigger's lawyer nodded at the plaster cast. He coughed politely, looking directly at Mother. "Furthermore, each of the females is willing to confirm that my client's dick is not only gigantic--- but good as hell on top of that." He sat back into his chair. "Those are not my words, but theirs."

"You bring them lying assed hoes to court, and my lawyer will expose their dirty, filthy lies, won't you?" She glared at her attorney.

"I'll do my best."

"You'll do your best," Mother fumed. "What kind of shit is that for a motherfucking lawyer to say. For goodness sake, show some fucking enthusiasm."

51

"Please contain yourself. I'm a professional," Mother's lawyer said, "you'll get your money's worth and then some. I promise you that."

The other lawyer was ready to end the meeting. "So we are going to Court?"

"Is pussy good?" Mother responded.

Both of the concerned parties prepared for Court. It was on.

One serious thing that surfaced on the very first day of Court was the Judge. He was mean.

"Young Lady," he admonished Mother from the bench, "I'll have you know that I'll not tolerate that sort of unbecoming attire in this honorable Court, especially from someone who is a party to the issue involved in dispute." He gazed down at Mother. "That dress is absolutely inappropriate."

"I don't think so, your Honor," Mother pleaded. "Under the current circumstances, I feel it's appropriate."

"You do?"

"Yes sir, this whole case is about sex, so well I----."

"Young Lady, for your information," the Judge interceded, "it is the facts that will be on display here, not your legs. Do you understand?"

"Yes sir."

"Good, because I will give you until tomorrow to find suitable attire."

The very next day, Court commenced.

"And how old are you?"

"Old enough, and woman enough to get away from a man with an itty-bitty dick."

The Judge flinched. "Must you be so graphic?"

Mother looked around the courtroom. "Ain't nothing up in here but grown folks, so I'm quite sure ain't nobody in here that don't know about the birds and the bees. What's the problem?"

The Judge sighed. "There is a certain amount of decorum that attaches to a courtroom."

"That's understandable," Mother replied, "and I intend to conduct myself in a ladylike fashion." She touched her hair lovingly. "How do you like my dress, your Honor?"

52

"As I was saying, these proceeding that take place in this honorable Court, and any other court in this country must be respected and held to a high standard, and as a Judge I will insist that everyone involved conduct himself or *herself* in a civilized manner." The Judge glared over the top of his spectacles. "Does everyone understand?"

In the moments that followed, silently prodded on by amateur courtroom enthusiasts and professional gossip-seekers, Mother solemnly recounted the tragic ordeal of being let down in the honeymoon suite.

"I was crushed," Mother groaned. "I had such high expectations, had dreamed of what a night like that was supposed to mean. All my life," Mother sobbed, "I have been led to believe that this was the night that all little girls spend their adult lives getting ready for, and then after finally finding the man I thought was worth the wait, he turns out to be a dud." Mother stifled another sob. "I guess I'll never be the same."

In the end, Mother took the traditional task of testifying, and transformed it into an intimate, bedtime story. She magically shifted the original purpose of a trial, which is to decide facts, into an open house forum on how good pussy functions, and what happens to the mind of a woman when a man's 'thang' malfunctions.

"I damned near went crazy."

In the end, the silly nigger conceded to a divorce. Mother had already gotten a pretty penny from the general store and house, and now with what she was awarded in Court, we were what she called 'niggers so rich our shit won't stink.'

I, personally, wondered how much money that took.

C H A P T E R   6

Even with money to burn, it was no small thing. Characteristically, I stopped being humanly productive as soon as the intoxication with being 'different' began. My softening was breathtakingly dramatic. Swift.

More precisely, I began to understand that implicit in these transformations was the explicit knowledge that I wouldn't forever be able to change back and forth. Pretty soon, unless I could delay it, I would be compelled to stop jumping the tracks between either/or, and remain steadfast to either one or the other.

On impulse, I believed that the gap would have to be bridged by necessity, and deep within, this severely frightened me. What were my choices? The fear was real, and my choices were earth-shattering because I had no earthly clue what it might take to meet the coming needs of what being different would induce.

I had learned nothing from my initial contact with the wafer-thin boy other than that I had enjoyed playing with fire, but what else was new? This pronouncement had been only a simple suspicion awaiting approval to remove its mask and become truth.

What did annoy me though was how easily I had survived being away from the wafer-thin boy. I wasn't consumed by any raging desires to hang myself, or to fling myself into the path of a speeding locomotive. Instead, despite my inexperience at missing anyone, I knew that I had inherited the ability to respond to goodbye with such ease from my Mother. Who else?

I remember hearing Mother school the Other Woman. "Girl, one man ain't nuthin' but a diplomat for another."

I shuddered at the memory, but it wasn't long before I had carried out an occasion to go hunting, or as Mother called it "nigger hunting".

I shivered inside. In the year between then and now, I had grown. Not a growth accented so much by massive proportions, but one defined by my genetic code's exquisite attention to detail. Mother's good looks had translated well. I was now a bonafide pretty boy.

Mother continually teased my brother and me. "If y'all nappy-headed niggers don't love me now, y'all sho' as hell will when y'all start getting all that pussy I know y'all gonna be getting with y'all fine, red asses. And don't neither one of you ever forget that the reason y'all so damned pretty is because of me. I make pretty babies."

Even though I was a rookie nigger hunter, I never once pooh-poohed the notion that I would not be successful. After all, I did possess Mother's genes, and she was a sexual predator par excellence.

At any rate, I found him almost without looking, but also found that he was impaired by the illusion that he was so incredibly desirable, so obviously hot that he merited undivided attention. He was indeed tantalizing despite the fact that he was fertilized with vanity.

"I want to kiss you," he explained to me as we sat alone in his car, "but I'm afraid for your safety."

"Why?" I asked.

"I might melt you."

I cursed under my breath.

"You still got milk behind your ears," he cooed. "Betcha ain't even started cumming yet." He kissed my hand. "I'm not sure if it's appropriate for me to turn you on because when I get through with you, you might go and cut your dick off or something." He rubbed my thigh. "After I get through with you, you certainly wouldn't find much need for it."

Out on this first encounter, I was beginning to find that hearing his own voice was one of his greatest devices when he needed to pleasure himself. I saw this as a grave insult to the reason I was where I was, and though I didn't desire the notoriety, this nigger was either going to fuck or fight. No ifs, ands, or buts about it. In the end, I left him with a bloody nose, and a lacerated lip. I also developed the terrible need to fight again.

To be absolutely and brutally candid, I felt bubbly as I marched into the seedy, dilapidated gym. It was shortly after sunset, a fortnight since my attack upon the pompous pretty boy in his red 'bed on wheels'.

The insides of the gym resembled a burned out garrison where heavy bags hung from the ceiling, and full length, scratched-up mirrors were pasted to the sweaty walls. No space really appeared empty as something or someone was forever moving in and out of the various shadows that haunted every crevice of the building.

Young boys crowded together on a mat performed leg raises. I stepped across them, quickly encountering a tall, skinny, yellow man, and his older, snaggled-tooth brother who showed his disciples how to stick and move. Beyond this pair was a trio of hopefuls who carefully watched as a fourth boxer jumped rope.

The density of the thick sweat disgusted me as I crossed over a hard, plank floor to the ring. When the pudgy, old trainer spotted me out of the corners of his eyes, he cursed without turning his head.

"What the fuck you want?"

I wanted to sound impressively tough. "The same thang anybody else wants who comes into a gym."

He turned slightly; only a fraction, though.

"I want to be a champion."

Now he turned full -face. The movement was surprisingly swift and cat-like. "Just like that," he snapped his fingers. "A fucking champion. No beginning, no middle, just a fucking champion." He pushed his finger into my nose, "It's snot-nose punks like you that makes my ass tired. Come in heah, smelling your own musk for the first time, and all of a sudden, you wanting to be a man. Well, if you intent on being a man, I'm gonna give you a piece of advice." He mugged me softly, pushing my head backwards. "Ain't but two things to do when you young and you feel yo' sap rising. You either get yo' first piece of pussy, or you get into yo' first fight, and judge from yo' puny ass, I advise you to go out and fuck something 'cause personally, I don't think you got the heart to be no fucking fighter." He punched me in the chest. "Just to show you that I ain't the most heartless motherfucker in the world, I'm gonna do yo' red ass a big favor. I don't owe you shit, but I'm gonna do it anyway." He

56

cupped my chin roughly in a viselike grip with his left hand. "And you had better 'preciate the shit out of it 'cause it will save yo' life just as sho' as penicillin cures the clap." He yelled for an assistant. "Bring me the instructions."

Seconds later, an almost elegant man with a stub of a cigar between his teeth, thrust a dingy sheet of paper at me.

"Can you read, red nigger," the trainer said menacingly.

"What the fuck you think?" I shot back.

"Jest in case you can't, read my lips. These are instructions on how to get yo' first shot of pussy. It says: 'buy candy for girl. Give candy to girl. Beg girl to take off her clothes for mo' candy. Once girl's clothers are off, ask her to open her legs. Then you take out yo' dick, and insert it between her open legs. You then begin to fuck. End of instructions." He tapped his head. "I done laid it all out for you. Now, don't get me wrong, I ain't got nuthin' 'gainst you, but you ain't no fighter. And you never will be, so get the fuck out of my gym."

Without preamble, I delivered a vicious one-two punch to his belly, and what I instantly noticed besides how rock hard his stomach muscles were was how deathly silent the gym became. At that moment, I clearly understood the preference of every swinging dick in the place. They wanted to slay me.

"Well, well," the trainer rasped, circling me like a vulture, sizing me up. "I see you stupid on top of everything else you might be. What you wanna hit me for, punk?"

"I ain't no punk, and if you don't like it, I'll hit you again but this time, it'll be in your mother-   fucking face."

The trainer laughed openly, greyish spit spewing off his cracked, stained teeth, "You will, will you?"

"Damn right."

"That won't make you tuff. It'll make you stupid."

"You think I give a fuck, but it will make you careful 'bout how you run your mouth to people."

The trainer's mouth grew twisted. "Put the gloves on him."

The boxing gloves seemed deceptively heavy, and the boxing ring was bathed in a soft glow that carried a deep aura of darkness. My corner, my stool, stood far to the right. This was not the steel cage where inexperience and fear could be compensated for by the fact there were no rules. In the steel cage, I could kick, bite, punch; anything. But here, with rules, I would have to bring my rage into a more narrow restraint. My focus would have to be sharper as I would be constrained to attempt destruction with only the use of my padded hands.

From memory, the trainer conjured up the boy most likely to do the most bodily harm to me without it looking as if I had bet set upon by a pack of rabid wolves.

He, my hand-chosen, destroyer, danced into the ring, sliding gracefully through the ropes, his sleek, black body already aglow with a thin glistening sweat.

In the near silence, the sounds of his shadow-boxing, the hissing in and out of his breath; the rapid, tat-a-tat tap of his foot upon the canvas, produced a darkly sinister narrative to the atmosphere, already swollen with the sensation of someone dying. Still, I couldn't bring myself to rip off the gloves, and then to tear out of the gym, running , not looking back; afraid. Cowardice, I was sure, would interfere with the rest of my life, and I needed no aid in breaking my total existence down into a marvel of day-to-day hell.

No, I would pay whatever price had to be paid for this personal self-examination. And he would pay dearly for teaching me.

I found myself on the canvas almost immediately. I was scalded with embarrassment as everyone howled in laughter as I lie on the canvas, balled up in a tight knot as if awaiting to get stomped. I forgot where I had been, remembered where I was, and got to my feet. Knowing it would take some time for my head to clear, I crudely pranced out of the intimate reach of his trip-hammer left hand.

He pursued me in earnest. It was as if he truly believed that an object, if hit hard enough, enough times would succumb. His quick, non-stop punches combined to elicit from me strong, tell-tale images of irreversible brain damage. I was shook. I had two more quick affairs with his left hand, but I managed to remain married to my senses. I did not fall down, but a badly blurred vision of me getting knocked out served to remind me to stay away from his punches so I wouldn't keep getting nailed by them.

I shuffled off-course to his right, just in time to avoid detection by a well-guided uppercut. Sensing that I was sick and tired of being hit only made him more bolder and more daring as he fired off blows from every which way, smashing my face with rights and lefts that originated from every imaginable angle. Still, I kept standing. He smote me with a punch that I didn't recognize was legal, and suddenly he began to fade in and out of focus. I was saved by the bell.

In the second round, I emerged partially from the fog of semi-consciousness, and tagged him with a few non-lethal punches. They didn't actually hurt, but they were infectious. I hit him some more. These blows, while they failed to purchase anything substantial for me by way of instilling fear or respect into my opponent, it was much better than getting hit.

I hit him again. "I think we understand each other now" I said through clenched teeth before swinging again.

He danced smoothly alongside the right side of the blue corner of the ring, and I pursued him like a loyal puppy dog. We exchanged blows, and my heart almost stopped. His punches didn't hurt any more, so I deliberately took one on the chin to test the theory.

He popped me with a crisp jab. I smiled. The round ended.

At the beginning of the final round, I sensed that I did not have to lose. He almost instantly changed my mind as he fired off a barrage of countless punches that upon landing flush upon my jaw, sounded slightly musical. However, I held him at bay with a crunching right hand that moved him backwards and sideways at the same time. His legs almost lost their commission, and at one minute, twenty-three seconds into the round, I finally did it. I knocked him down!

As his back spread upon the canvas, his dark face mirrored an odd assortment of chain-link expressions. They whizzed across his face, causing his mouth to gesture noiselessly, curving his lips over and under his teeth.

He was up and about quickly, swirling around me impatiently before eventually settling down into a flat-footed stance. He intended to load up and to move in. A solid left hook, preceded by a fledgling left jab blurred his vision, stalling his plans to demolish me. These blows stipulated that I wasn't to be fucked with, and to make sure my hands weren't speaking in tongues, I crashed an overhand right to the base of his temple. The motherfucker understood.

Overcome with confidence, I endeavored to kill him. His wobbling head became the visual centerpiece of my preoccupation as I dumped buckets of jabs into, upon, and upside it until in less than a few seconds, it came to symbolize how vicious, cruel, and utterly merciless I could be.

To minimize his potential to recover, I elbowed him in the nose when we clenched. It was a dirty tactic to be sure, but I was smelling blood. I waded in. Since acquiring the ability to be hit with startling regularity, he was dumbfounded, and he looked even dumber as he fell through space, lying horizontally in the prone position of having bitten off more than he could chew.

I raised my hands in victory and snarled like a wounded beast. Everyone was scared shitless.

.Once a boxer exists, he lives to become a champion, and out of the lot at the gym where I now trained, everyone knew that I was the prize candidate. After the beating at my hands, the kid who seemed destined to be a golden gloves champion, floundered badly, losing to guys not even his equal.

In most quarters, it was whispered that I had beat him out of his heart, I didn't know about that. Or care. If he got his ass beat, he got his ass beat. It was none of my concern. I just wanted to fight my way through the amateurs, claim the Golden Gloves, and perhaps earn a spot on the Olympic squad in three years. And that wasn't asking much from someone with the potential and talent I possessed.

"You the best damn fighter I ever seen," the trainer confessed, "and If you don't get too-pigheaded, you can be the heavyweight champion of the world."

On average, I fought far fewer rounds in competition than anyone else because I normally beat them senseless within the first two minutes of the round. I had become a monster.

I was shaking in my boots. It felt strangely as if all the blood in my head was clotting, layering my brain with spoiled cottage cheese. I couldn't think, could only barely see, and had no idea what to do or say. Thank God for Mother. Despite how golden silence was, it served no real purpose when a young man is supposedly consumed in his first real courtship. Mother had, I noticed, been watching us---the girl and I--- with considerable interest.

Coming to my rescue, she offered the girl a glass of fruit punch. She politely begged the girl's pardon, and then whispered in my ear.

"That's a fine piece of ass there, my son."

I nodded dumbly.

"And one thing a girl always remembers is her first dick." She smiled, winking naughtily. "Always stays on her mind. Now, get to work." She touched my shoulder maternally. "Be first," she chanted. "Ain't that what they tell you in the gym?"

"Yeah, but," I started to protest.

"Ain't no different. Be first", she coached. "Be first."

"What was that all about?" the pretty girl asked once I was back in her company.

"You know how Mothers are."

She giggled. "Let's dance."

The song was too damned long, and I felt extremely silly trying to imitate the strange moves everyone else on the dance floor was doing. As the trumpet finally blared its last note, I literally dragged her to the punch bowl, and quickly filled a pair of glasses. I handed her one. Soon, she would have to piss. That much was sure. And I could use the time to figure out how to keep doing the little stupid shit that made these little bitches say yes when their parents asked them if that they had fun.

Across the room, I spotted Mother. She was watching me---us--- over the top of a glass of something other than fruit punch. She made it obvious that she saw me---us---. She waved.

I put my arm around the pretty girl's waist, and escorted her back to our table which Mother had made sure was darkly secluded. She really wanted me to fuck this girl.

And then what?

This puzzled the shit out of me. Even more puzzling was how in the world Mother had reached the conclusion that I wanted to build an empire with my dick, the way she had amassed one with her pussy. But then again, I knew. Money married money. We were rich, the pretty girl's family was rich, but if the two families wanted to put the fucking money

61

under one name, why didn't Mother just do what she was so fucking good at---breaking up happy marriages, and then running off with the man.

"This ain't about fucking, nigger,' Mother would explain later, "it's about eating. Ain't got shit to do with the brass bed, stupid. This is about the silver spoon."

At a handful of minutes before the hour, Mother stormed towards me. I could tell she was upset. It was as though she felt the pretty girls' pussy would turn into a cabbage if I didn't get it before the clock struck twelve.

"Here," she ordered, "drink this down."

I obediently put the glass to my lips and tasted the murky-colored brew. "Ma," I protested.

"Drink it, nigger."

I downed the bourbon is a single gulp.

Immediately, the barrier that separated my bashfulness evaporated in the fiery alcoholic haze. The drink sizzled my insides, warming me up like a liquid radiator. In a few minutes, I was eager to dance again. I brazenly marched the pretty girl to the center of the dance floor, and danced with reckless abandon.

Actually, I didn't dance. I merely let loose, and did what I did at the gym. I shadow-boxed to the beat. It stopped everyone in their tracks. They stared at me as I beat the air with a dazzling array of hooks and jabs. They clapped and this urged me on, compelling me to reach for even greater abandon.

They clapped. This urged me on, insisting that I reach for even greater abandon, and I sought it with every ounce of all that I was. I felt stimulated. When the music stopped, they still wouldn't let me quit. The rhythm of my unrestrained animal passion pounded and thundered between my ears, and the bass line of my unrefined freedom stimulated me like a drug of heavenly proportions. Epic shit.

I danced myself to life, and when I collapsed in a sweaty heap on the floor, their applause was deafening. They loved me.

"You were great," the pretty girl gushed.

"Will you be my girlfriend?" I responded.

"*Girlfriend?!*" It was Mother was had appeared magically. "Girlfriend is such a misleading title," she preached. "You want her to be your woman, don't you, son?" Mother smiled. "She can only be a girlfriend to a boy, and I'm in the habit of raising men." She winked at me. "Now, get it right this time," she half-joked before walking away,

We experienced instant maturity.

"Would you be my woman?"

"Of course," the pretty girl replied. "I would love to."

Years later, I would wonder what the devil got ahold of my tongue that night and made me ask that. Oh, the peril of strong drink.

According to my own research, I was now entombed in a social environment where money was the yardstick by which everything else was measured. In a sense, this was a black mecca, a wealthy microcosm of what white folks yearned for, killed for, died for, and leaped out of windows for.

Here, we had it all. In this small dimly-lit metropolis existed unparalleled ease. We resided amongst samples and examples of all the sensual attractions that made it a great honor to be one of the 'haves.' Few families had made it to where we were now in so quick a time, and Mother never let us forget it.

On the other side of this exquisite finery was the fact that Mother viewed my boxing as primitive, unworthy of someone of my social status.

"We're still in the process of moving up," Mother scolded me on a number of occasions, "and it doesn't look well if you go around beating people up. The stupid fact that it's legal and licensed doesn't add any glamor to it." She huffed disdainfully. "That's what poor niggers do, and you have no reason to want to imitate those savages. That's why I always fail to mention it when I discuss you."

"Don't be discussing me, then."

"And that's the thanks I get? After all these years of faithful service to you, and this is how you repay me? Most niggers would be damn glad to have a Mama like me, and would be glad to do anything she asked."

I burst out laughing.

"What, I look like a clown or something?" She put her hands on her hips, and made a funny face. Then she turned dead serious. "The last thing I need is for some gold-digging bitch to end up in your bed, trying to steal all this good shit right out from under your nose."

"Don't worry, Mama, that ain't gonna happen to neither me or my brother."

Mother patted my cheek in concern. "You still too young to grasp how seriously bitches take security." She shook her head sadly. "What they'll do to you is a thousand times worse than what any man could do to you inside that boxing ring." She playfully mugged me. "Boy, remember that a good woman in bed is a far worse killer than a bad man in the ring." This time, she embraced me warmly. I got scared.

Suddenly, I realized that not much of what Mother had done had been entirely for fun and performance. She had always been concerned with getting us to the top of the mountain, and she had succeeded, and she done it, perhaps joining a long list of women who had forged an empire from the economy of good pussy.

My trainer was getting spooked by the bold luxury of my home environment, feeling it was a threat to my hunger and drive to be a champion.

"How the fuck you gonna stay mean and tuff when you sleeping on silk sheets. It don't take no prophet to see that inside of a year, you gonna be as soft as candy. Boy, you standing too close to all the frilly shit that makes niggers weak." He groaned. "I worry 'bout you."

In all actuality, there was no real need to. I beat the living shit out of all my opponents, easily grabbing The Golden Gloves Championship in my weight class. I had arrived.

Nonetheless, by now, the pretty girl was starting to distress me. She was tired of being a virgin.

"I need some relief," she told me one day.

"What?!"

"If we don't fuck soon, I'm going to burst wide open. What are we waiting for, anyway? You've done what you said you wanted to do which was to win golden gloves." She rubbed my thigh suggestively. "You have proved what you can do to men. Now, show me what you can do to a woman."

I almost gagged. She sounded just like Mother!

"Put me on my back," she teased, "and you had better keep me down there longer than for a ten count."

"We don't have enough privacy," I pleaded weakly. "I'll come up with something soon," I lied.

"You know we can do it at your house. Your Mama is always gone."

"I ain't never did it before, have you?"

Quicker than a cat, her hand flew to my face.

"Why you do that?"

"Boy, you know my pussy is still new, now, don't you?"

"Yeah, but that means it's gonna hurt."

"Then, you should be good at it," she purred. "Don't boxers get paid to hurt people?"

I exploded in laughter. "That's the dumbest comparison I ever heard tell of."

She laughed, then stopped. "I'll be over your house at nine."

Pussy-fiends will forever declare throughout all eternity that the first piece of pussy is always the best, but judging from what I felt afterwards, much of the ballyhooed glory must have passed me by. At least, that was my original assessment.

Then she wanted to do it again.

Fortunately, strength was beginning to trickle back into my limp body which felt tired and drained. Shamelessly, the pretty girl reached between my legs and gently stroked me, softly kneading the flesh of my inner thigh. At once, a powerful surge of passion overwhelmed me, the sheer depth of it life-altering. I took her, and I became her hero.

I drove her purposely hard, and now that we had acquired an intimate feel for one another, we made no sacrifices. Time, for example, became meaningless. Space, as we had previously known it, no longer existed. Nothing needed to be explained or understood. We just were.

Of course, it had to end, but when it did, it was with a delicious finality that threaded the nimble balance between ending and transformation.

While she slept, her head resting upon my shoulder, I tried to shun the look-alike emotions that littered themselves into my brain that were left there by the wafer-thin boy. I had loved him too. Granted, the feelings were thinner and less defined, but they were by no means awkward aberrations. I had loved him, and that had not seemed complicated at all then.

But now?

Maybe, I had been mistaken. Maybe that was lust. *And this was love*. Perhaps, the feelings I had experienced with the wafer-thin boy were just wildly popular gizmos, something beautiful to fit into the tricky category of my budding sexuality until I found my true niche.

At that point in time, I had no idea if it would pay to push away all my previously-held concepts of love, and just wait for whatever came next with the pretty girl. Could she trick whatever it was in me that made me want to spend the rest of my life on the other side of the sexual fence to leave me alone? Could she defuse the desire? Could good pussy be that good---or strong?

Anyway, for the moment, this felt so right.

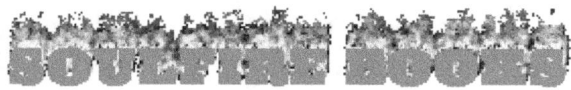

At the expiration of another fifty-two weeks, I had managed to string together another impressive bunch of victories in the ring that once more culminated with me winning The Golden Gloves Championship a second time. Needless to say, scarcely anyone was surprised.

Dazzling personal success kindled in me the explosive desire to believe devoutly that wanting to be different had run its course, that I had survived the windfall of wanting to stick my nose into perversion; alas, that I would fall into the abyss.

But, all too often, fate comes along.

It was way past quitting time in the gym, but I was in no particular mood to leave. After I had showered, I merely stood alone in a musty corner, observing dusk putting on its dark mascara. I would soon enter this darkness invented by the depreciation of light.

Around the corner from the gym, I spied the elegant man's car. At about that same time, I noticed that he was not alone in the vehicle. Even from a distance, I could distinctly tell that the other passenger was male which meant that they shouldn't have been doing what they were doing.

From where I was, I couldn't be seen so I saw no risk in watching from an even better vantage point, so I crept closer. My breath caught in my throat. *They were kissing!* Two men.

They continued to kiss in a perversely seductive, open-mouthed kiss that even the wafer-thin boy and I had not tried. From the way their heads were twisting and turning, it was absolutely clear that neither of the pair was attempting to mislead the other about how much they were enjoying it.

As soon as I got close enough to see it all, the elegant man fired up the Caddy, driving off to leave me standing in the cold of the darkness. I shivered.

Seeing what I shouldn't have seen caused me to relapse a few days later. I was visibly plagued by the desire to let the elegant man kiss me, or better yet to introduce me to the young man he had been kissing.

After days and nights of internal chaos, I almost found the courage to confront the elegant man with the report of my voyeurism, but I didn't. The results: I was miserable. I wanted in. I wanted to be a welcomed member of the club, but I knew of no tactical way to do so without informing the elegant man that I had deliberately invaded his privacy, and after this to confess that I, too, shared his attraction and fascination with men.

Surprisingly, and perhaps shockingly, nothing was going wrong between me and the pretty girl. I continued to fuck her with gusto; however under the present circumstances of me loving her, I still didn't feel healed. For all practical purposes, it was as if I was simply counting down the days until I had made all the necessary adjustments that would allow me to cross over-----completely. And for some reason, I didn't want to wiggle out of this one.

Another week passed, and it was on the eve of the umpteenth time that I had fallen short of asking the elegant man to love me. I was not reckless enough just to barge into his office, blurt the whole story out, and threaten his ass with blackmail if he refused to introduce me into his world of secrets and smokescreens. Either way, I could get into loads of trouble. I could be hounded out of boxing, could earn the disrespect of my woman, and worse of all, raise the ire of Mother.

Mother!

The first thing to know was that, as far as possible, I wanted to live both lives fully. And the next day it got easier. I was going to confront the elegant man. My mind was made up, and that was that, but as I drew near to his office, I heard his voice and realized that he was on the phone. I stopped short of the doorway and eavesdropped. Maybe he was talking to his young lover?

Aside from the unconcealed urgency in his voice, I was taken aback by how well he spoke when the language was not the 'gut-bucket-spit-and-cussing' jargon of the gym. Then he said something that weighed me down.

"Oh no," I whispered to myself. "not that again." Then I listened some more.

"One day," the elegant man declared, "the whole world will fear the power of The Talented 10th."

I   ran   away.

CHAPTER 7

Thinking back, I should have been more forward-thinking. Even though I knew I could get the pretty girl pregnant, I still hadn't examined the risks logically. At my age, who the fuck did. In my mind, the simple fact that I didn't envision her pregnant was enough of an incentive to keep right on fucking as though her pussy was endowed with enough sense to keep on dodging sperm.

At first, the pretty girl talked freely about her condition, but then grew more scared as she neared the point where she would begin to show. At that time, it would no longer be just our lil secret. At that time, it would become, quite simply, the talk of the town. We would undoubtedly become the youthful symbol of what happens to teenagers who go to school by day, and fuck like grown folks at night.

In the long term, I didn't want that shit. I was horrified, and without a second thought, developed a disgust for pussy. Too many strings were attached. The portfolio of pussy was mired in a hidden agenda that a nigger always ignored until he was banged upside the head with the news, "Baby, I'm pregnant!"

In any event, I wasn't wholly prepared to do something as drastic as giving a new-born nigger the chance to call me daddy. I had no desire to expose what could become of my life to what would become of my life if I let the pretty girl have this bastard child, compelling me to answer for it.

Fuck Fatherhood!

I went off to see the wizard, or at least his ghetto equivalent----- my boxing coach.

Years of listening to Mother had convinced me irrevocably that there were a thousand ways to tell a lie, but only one way to tell the truth: simply don't lie.

"I fucked this girl," I said casually, "and now she's knocked up. What am I supposed to do?"

"Whatta fuck you mean, whatta you do? You start acting like a daddy because that's what fucking will make you."

"But I don't want no baby."

The trainer roared with joyous laughter. "Too late for any regrets now. You see them boxing gloves you just took off, nigger. They are for protection, so that no matter how much you get carried away and try to kill your opponent, you can't 'cause you got on protection. Same thang with fucking bitches. You gotta wear your protective gear, dig?"

"But------."

"But, my ass, you silly motherfucker. That's what a dick rubber is all about."

"But------."

"But, nuthin,' nigger. You done turned a one night stand in a lifetime of getting up and going to some white man's job. You done let yo' stupid-assed dick put chains on yo' dumb ass. Whatever chances you may have had being a world champion just got squirted out of yo' dickhead, you dickhead."

When I recognized that I wouldn't be able to elicit any sympathy from the trainer, I started to bad-mouth him. "You ain't shit but a selfish old-assed man. You don't care about shit except boxing." I spoke spitefully. "There a whole lotta other shit going on in the world better than motherfuckers getting knocked out that you ain't trained right. You ain't shit."

"And it was done that way on purpose, you silly fool. I lived my life so that I wouldn't be shit. Oh, you think that being a piece of shit is the shit, right?" He scowled. "Shit is shit. Now, get the fuck out of my face."

I started to get missing.

"But before you go, remember this. I was wrong about you once before. I didn't believe that you had what it took to be a fighter, but you proved me wrong. Now, I don't think you have what it takes to be a man, but I can stand to be corrected if I'm wrong. Only thang is that this time, you can't beat me wit' yo' hands. No siree, this time, if you can do it, you gotta use yo' head." He chuckled sagely. Then he left.

I made the call around ten-thirty pm.

"Hello."

"I need to speak to you, man...bad."

"How did you get my number?"

"Why, you that important?"

"The point you're missing," The elegant man replied, "is that I don't like talking to someone on my personal phone who didn't have my number personally given to them."

"Don't get mad," I countered. "I was just joking with you."

"What is it that you called me about?"

"I can't talk about it over the phone."

"Why,' the elegant man said heatedly, "you think you that important?"

"Naw, man, it ain't nothing like that, but it does mean that if you come and pick me up, it will give me more time to think."

"Think!? Think about what. What you're going to say once I get wherever it is you want me to come?'"

"No, I already know what I'm gonna say. I just gotta find out where to start."

"Listen," the elegant man rasped wearily, "this is what I'm going to do."

"What?"

"Hang up."

"No, don't. Listen, I-I got this girl pregnant."

"And?"

"I saw you kissing a man."

"Where the hell are you, nigger?"

Within the hour, the Caddy pulled up to where I was wanting, and when I got in, I couldn't help but notice that the interior reeked of sex. By way of comparison, the scent was not as pronounced as when Mother and one of her lovers had been at it in the bedroom at home, but this

71

smell derived from the same origin, only more masculine. The sweaty stench filled the car. The elegant man had not been lonely tonight.

"What's with you," he growled. "Has boxing gotten so easy for you that you ready to try your hand at blackmail?" He looked disappointed with me. "Just what is it that you think you're going to get out of me by spreading a rumor like that?"

"It ain't no lie, so don't play like it is. I know what I saw, and I saw you kissing a man."

The elegant man fidgeted. "Have you mentioned this—what you thought you saw—to anyone else?"

"Not a motherfucking soul. I'm the only one that saw it, so I figure it ain't nobody else's business." The elegant man attitude changed once I had refreshed his memory, and by the time I had finished, his eyes were no longer casting darts at me, and he was greatly relieved that I had not spread his dirty laundry all over the gym. I made him feel lucky and took the opportunity to let it be known that he owed me. "I saved your reputation," I boldly pointed out.

"I've been in worst situation," he shrugged nonchalantly. "More than likely, I would have weathered the storm." The elegant man wearily looked out of the car's window. "But what do I owe you in return for your graciousness?"

Another thing I had learned from Mother was that when you were in dire straits, gimmicks don't usually work, so I laid my cards on the table. "I fucked this girl, got her pregnant, and now I want to get her fixed."

The elegant man laughed. "*Fixed!* You made it sound like she a fucking horse or some barnyard animal. *Fixed!*" he once more laughed. "What do you know about this kind of woman fixing?"

I licked my lips nervously. "Nuthin', but I know they still do it."

"Listen to me well." He pointed his finger in my face threateningly. "You definitely have your people mixed up if you think I'm interested in helping you to commit a crime. I don't owe you shit, and just because you a big, bad nigger down at the gym, you stupid if you think you can blackmail me into helping you. What I do is my own business. I'm an adult, and the world is not that small that I couldn't move away from here and to find another place to live where I could do what the fuck I choose to without people peeking into my car window." He looked me in the eyes. "If you want me to commit a crime with you, the least you could

72

have done is to have asked me to knock over a liquor store with you. This way, at least, I would have gotten something out it."

"You'll get something out of this."

"Nigger, pleeze," he croaked sarcastically.

I placed my hand firmly on his upper thigh, gazing steadily into his startled eyes. "I like what you like," I said, moving my fingers until I touched him.

He moaned.

"See what you'll be getting," I whispered softly as I slid closer, nuzzling his earlobe.

"Oh my goodness," the elegant man shrieked.

"How you like me now?"

"Welcome to the club," he blurted happily.

The abortion doctor lived south of the city in a privileged section of town where the air smelled honeysuckle sweet. Once we entered the far end of the city, the elegant man picked over wide avenues and tree-lined boulevards one by one as though he was choosing tomatoes in a grocery store until he found the one next to the church with the bell tower.

I held the pretty girl in my arms, consoling her, trying to convince her that we were doing the right thing and that all would be well. She shivered in my arms all the more. She was not impressed on either count and neither, quite frankly, was I.

"Well, this is it," the elegant man said grandly.

Around the back of the house, alongside the terrace, was an elevated walkway that climbed up to a glassed-in façade. A handsomely painted sign read: Doctor. Another sign directly beneath it read; OPEN.

"Well, this is it," the elegant man repeated.

Ignoring him, I brushed past and opened the door for the pretty girl, and once the three of us were in the office, no one seemed willing to do anything to draw attention to our presence. We stood mute, flinching self-consciously under the weight of the secret we shared and the enormous risk we were willing to take to rid ourselves of its burden.

The elegant man moved silently away from us as if to remove himself from our predicament. The move was also shrewdly designed to remind us---the pretty girl and me---that he was merely here to witness the murder and had not, in any way, played a role in the execution. The responsibility for that would fall upon our heads.

Afraid that my resolve would shrivel up like a raisin in the sun, I stepped to the desk and pressed the buzzer. Instantly, the doctor entered.

"Come this way." His instructions were cold. He looked stiff and formal in his white frock, gripping a gnarled clipboard that fluttered with official-looking paper. "You, two, are such a young couple." He stopped us at a brightly-lit waiting room. He smiled at the pretty girl sweetly. "You come with me." He turned to the elegant man, then to me. "I will return her to you in a minute." Then, as if we needed to know. "It's time for her examination."

"Examination?" the pretty girl sputtered.

"Nothing major," the doctor said casually, "but I must take some preliminary precautions to insure that all will go well and it will, don't you worry; however, I will need to determine just how far along you are and----."

"What or how great are the risks normally?" the elegant man quizzed.

The doctor frowned. "For a healthy woman, the risks----."

"But this is not a woman. She is a terribly frightened, young girl here at the urging of a young fool who is just as afraid as she is."

"Well, then, maybe it is the young fool who needs to be operated upon rather than his female companion."

The elegant man smiled tightly. "Even so, nothing that could be done to or upon him now will have any effect on what he has already done too her." He flashed me an evil eye. "Sometimes, the guilty do go unpunished."

"I take it, sir, that you have travelled far to get here. Don't you think it's a little late to start getting ethical?"

"It was never my ethics that were in question," the elegant man snapped. "I'm just an errand boy. This fool and his girlfriend needed a ride and someone they could trust."

"And a qualified doctor as well it seems."

"Most doctors I know don't practice by the light of the moon," The elegant man said stiffly.

"Must I remind you that you came to me. Since I do not openly advertise, it must have taken some considerable doing to locate me and yet here you are in my office, questioning me. You people---."

"You people, huh?"

"Don't take offense. It's not racial. I merely meant skeptics such as yourself, the naysayers. What I do is keep an already confused world from becoming overpopulated with those who don't belong here."

"Don't belong here," I blurted. "What is that supposed to mean?"

"I meant no offense, but there are some people that don't deserve to live. If I had my way, I would kill them------."

"I'll kill you," I screamed. "I'll kill you."

The elegant man stepped between me and the doctor.

"I will kill you," I repeated.

"I'm quite sure you would. If you can kill your own flesh and blood, then I have no doubt that you would indeed kill me."

"I grabbed the pretty girl by the arm and pushed her out of the door. "Fuck that motherfucker." I glanced back at the elegant man. "Let's go.

CHAPTER 8

By far, the greatest falsehood of my life had been that I could be a good father. Another one, equally as great, and as equally false was that I could live without Mother telling me what to do. Truth, in all its celibate purity, struck twice.

It was fall, and the seat of morning was being warmly heated by a playful sun. I felt temporarily out of sorts for reasons that I couldn't assemble into a logical explanation, so I tucked away my foreboding sense of dread and smiled widely.

I simply stared at my new=born son, unable to answer, but as a gesture, I kissed his tiny, red face when the pretty girl lovingly stuffed him into my trembling arms.

"That ain't how you hold no baby," Mother scolded. "That ain't no loaf of bread." She placed him smugly into my arms. "Ain't that tiny, lil nigger fine." She beamed, looking at me. "This should be the happiest day of your life."

Then my whole world ended.

Mother was arrested!

In their senseless devotion to being good cops, they snatched my son from Mother's loving arm, and clamped the handcuffs on her.

"We have an outstanding warrant for your arrest for the charge of murder," one of the lawmen commented acidly.

Towards the beginning of the next ten seconds, my mind would neither process nor receive information. The hospital room in the maternity ward grew exceptionally smaller and oxygen-starved while my initial response was to go for the gun of the nearest cop and blast all of them to pieces. But I didn't move. I couldn't, and from that moment onward, it would long be a matter of wonder why neither my brother nor I didn't fight that day, and die to defend our Mother's honor even though she was as guilty as sin.

After all she had done for us.

At one point as they were removing Mother from the hospital room, I winked at my brother as if to say, "Mother will prevail." I don't know if he bought it or not, but he winked back. Once Mother was placed into the back of the black and white squad car, the very first thing I recognized was that my son had just became an impediment.

This was no joke. Whatever lurked ahead of right now would not be filled with fun and games, and it sure would be no way to start a family or to begin a new life. I prayed the pretty girl wouldn't sense my arrogance or my agony, but Mother came first.

"I'm leaving you, bitch," I boldly stated, and if that was out of her reach of comprehension, I added, "now!" Feeling that the very least I could do would be to provide a reasonable explanation for my exit, so I did. "I don't need no bitch and no baby getting in my way. It's always been just me, Mother, and my brother, and that's how it's always gonna be, and ain't shit you can say or do that's gonna change that."

Sometimes, traditions change.

Quicker than a flash we were out of the hospital, and into Mother's new Buick. When she had purposely dropped the key purposely on the bed, I knew, without thinking, what that meant.

I was a good driver.

So many times when we had set off in the dead of the night to get away from someone Mother was tired of, or had used up, she taught me how to drive so I could participate more directly in out get-away. Whenever she would get tired of driving, I would take over behind the wheel while Mother climbed into the backseat to sleep.

"Mama," I used to ask at first, "Where do you want me to go?"

This would always annoy her. "Nigger, do you know where you are now?"

"No ma'am."

"Good," she would snap, "Because that means you're lost, don't it?"

"Yes ma'am."

"Then you going in the right direction, nigger, because we trying to stay lost so the farther you go not knowing where you are, the better. Now, shut up, and drive."

Jolted back to reality, I first stopped off at the house and looted it for whatever money was available, and then I was off into whatever would come next with my brother, my woman, and my son.

Off we went, and one of the first things I noticed as we clambered into town was the absence of the noonday hum. In its place was a sullen curtain of puckered, swollen silence. Home, it seemed, had been purged of hope as it nestled quietly, mourning itself. It was a welcome that frazzled my nerves.

It was something other than the pangs of nostalgia that drew me slowly through the streets because I sensed something more tragic. I parked in front of the Other Woman's house, and even from the sidewalk, the house seemed cold. The windows were dark. Something was amiss.

Most of the steps that led up to the front yard were old, hewed out of grey brick, but many were new, carved from real granite. They all rose up to an enclosed garden that sported azaleas in spring, but now festered with a dull, withered brown.

The Other Woman rushed from the house to greet us. She fell upon my brother and me, showering us with hugs and kisses, squeezing us both into her loving arms.

"I have missed y'all so much," she cried. "So much. There hasn't been a day that has gone by when I didn't think of my boys. Oh, Lord, I missed my babies."

"We missed you, too," I told her truthfully. "It's really good to see you again." I looked around. "Where's Mama? Didn't she get out this morning?"

"And who is this young Princess, and just who is the little bundle of joy?"

I made the introductions. "Where's Mama?"

My brother and I waited anxiously.

"Let's go inside," The Other Woman offered.

"Don't tell me they denied her bail?" I remarked angrily. "They did the same thing the last time. When can we go see her?"

The Other Woman burst into tears. "Please. Everybody, let's just go inside. Please."

Several features of the house suggested that nothing had really changed since we had last been here, but still the prevailing mood and

78

atmosphere was one of dark gloom. When we were being seated in the living room, the sense of something being wrong was so terribly suffocating that I was unable to speak or breathe. My brother was likewise afflicted. After a lengthy silence, the pretty girl spoke firmly. "Where is their Mother?"

Once more, The Other Woman sobbed.

"Mama!?" I screamed. "What has happened to Mama?"

"She's…..she's dead. She hung herself in her jail cell this morning."

I   thought   I   would   scream   forever.

CHAPTER 9

I soon found out that the probation officer was himself engaged in a furious life and death battle which partially accounted for the sickly way he looked at Mother's funeral. He had cancer and that explained everything.

Out of some sense of misguided duty, I began to visit him regularly once he was confined to his home. Needless to say, I did not enjoy this unnecessary exposure to the carnage of cancer's slow taking-of-life, but I continued to visit. Maybe it was because I somehow sensed that he was dying to tell me something of great importance. Therefore I came, I went. I came back.

And then one day.

"Did you ever enjoy the other side?" he asked.

I didn't flinch. "Yes."

"Was it a bright spot for you, or are you now opposed to it?"

"I have no regrets, if that's what you want to know."

"Good. I'm pleased to hear that, but let me ask you something." He formed a bridge with his fingers. "What if I had a heart filled with love and let's say that I offered it to a beautiful young woman who rejected it. Now, say I then offered this same genuine love to a man, would my love, all of a sudden, become trashy? It's the same love that knows no boundaries, but it is the dictates of society that determines who will ultimately benefit from my love."

"I see what you're saying, and yes, it is wrong."

"Well, what are you going to do about it?"

"Me?!"

"Yes," he pointed at me, staring intently. "Are you going to act boldly, or are you going to hide in the closet?"

"This is America. I can do as I please. I'm a human being."

"Don't jump to any conclusions, Mr. Human Being." He shook a finger in my face. "Are you blind? How can you call yourself a human when you live in America? The color of your skin has robbed you of being a man, and the fact that you have slept with one has robbed you of being human." He was angry. "Come back tomorrow."

"Bitch!" I screamed at the pretty girl, "the next time you just gonna lay there like a knot on a log, please let me know in advance. Fucking ain't supposed to be no do-it-yourself kinda thang. You supposed to help."

"I told you before we got started that I wasn't in the mood, and you decided to go ahead like you didn't care about my feelings at all."

"I could understand if you had a headache or a stomachache, but to tell a nigger that you ain't in the mood takes the cake."

"Go to sleep, sweetie," the pretty girl cooed. "I'm not in the mood for arguing either."

Within minutes, she was fast asleep, buried beneath the covers with her back to me. Even though I was slightly upset, I didn't wish to encourage or introduce any drama into our relationship. I really loved the pretty girl, and we both believed and understood that our constant fucking would give birth to a more sophisticated way of dealing with each other as we grew older. At the moment, fucking dominated merely every aspect of our lives because in our youthful glee, it was what worked. Later, we would build on whatever experiences fucking provided, and round out the rest of our lives in bliss.

Without a doubt, I was convinced that pussy, with all its elaborate mystery, endowed a woman with a sacred splendor that no right-minded man could resist, but I was not always in the right mind, so there were times when I was attracted to menfolk.

Now, was one such time.

Even though I had yet to be initiated into the local gay scene, thanks to the probation officer, I had a phone number.

"These are a close-knit, closed-mouth group," I had been warned. "Very discreet, and very professional, but once you're in, you become a part of a network that could be very beneficial in the future."

Needless to say, it wasn't the future I was concerned about when I phoned.

"Hello, I'm a friend of the probation officer."

"Ah, the young one. I have wondered when you would call, and I'm greatly pleased that you have. What can I do for you?"

"I'm bored."

"That's such an unnecessary condition. However, it can be easily remedied, if that is your choice." There was deep breathing. "Do you, my tender friend, desire release from the boredom you now entertain?"

I swallowed hard, excitement building. "Yes, I seek emancipation."

The voice seemed to smile. "You have no idea how happy you have just made me. Put on your dancing shoes, and I'll be there to pick up in thirty minutes.

"I stay-----"

"I know where you stay. We all do."

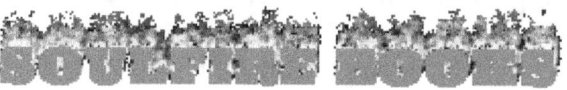

The pace of the music quickened, accelerating the frenzy, holding everyone captive. This was some place. It was part shrine, part burial chamber. I loved it. I threw myself into the celebration of raw lust, my sweat a dirty libation that my dance partner savored, a pungent nectar so heady that he licked me dry.

I had no idea where my clothes were. Guess what? I didn't give a damn. I was too fucking busy indulging in and enjoying all the stimulating pleasures of a new culture. I was a flower. There was so much to take in that I experienced a sort of visual overload that temporarily numbed my brain. I was passed around from table to table to be kissed, touched, and oogled. The entire panorama of sexual delights were laid bare before my very eyes, and in my youthful obsession to please myself, I cultivated an appetite that the pretty girl would no longer be able to sate.

The possession and use of my bodily orifices was given over to those who, after long years of study and education, personally excelled in the art of transforming that particular orifice into a fleshy shrine.

At times, I adopted the willing attitude of a sacrificial virgin; at other times, I assumed the role of a serpent-king, crawling into and sprawling over anyone I chose, but at all times, I felt free.

At sometimes before dawn, I went home.

The very next morning when I reported to my probation officer, he carefully weighed the reports of my behavior at my 'coming out' ball. For a number of seconds, his face was dissected and aligned with horizontal recesses where deep thoughts or concerns resided in the creases.

He said nothing.

Suddenly the rigid grid of furrows that had flowered in his wrinkled brows and cheeks vanished, and a partially happy smile was flying full-mast under his twinkling eyes. "Damn," he exclaimed, "seems like I missed a helluva party."

I agreed. "You sure as hell did.

He sighed, then turned serious. "Just the same, be careful. There is much more to your journey besides being a human sacrifice."

"Such as?"

He pointed at a desk drawer. "Look inside."

I extracted a legal document.

"Read it," I was commanded

Awareness of what I was reading and what it implied jolted me. "Are you crazy!?"

"I didn't expect that response," the probation officer said softly, "but to answer your question. No, I'm not crazy."

"Okay, then, why me?"

"Simple. Any time a group or organization is established, the man or men who found it always understand they are routinely apprentices; workers for someone who will come at a later time. Some far-sighted groups have even been started even before the hoped-for one is born, but that doesn't deter the workers. They simply labor on, holding the fort down until the real leader arrives." The probation officer sighed. "I know it all sounds mysterious, but practically every organization operates on the principle that its messiah is coming one day."

"And I imagine this is the reason why you put me in your will, and left everything to me, as some sort of inducement."

"Go home, pretty one, this has nothing to do with me leaving you a lot of money. It's more about the legacy you will leave behind you."

I was more than ready to go home.

For the probation officer, the next day brought bad news. His condition grew worse, the coughing now more severe. Everything seemed to deteriorate simultaneously. It was almost as if he was on a cliff inside his head, and had just leaped. He was falling slowly, yet surely, and once he hit the ground, he knew it would be all over. The probation officer was merely waiting to hit the ground.

On each visit, I watched him contending with death. He noticed my discomfort.

"The end is near."

I had to ask. "How does it feel?"

"What, death?"

I nodded.

"So unpretentious, so uncomplicated. Death is the prized fruit on the tree of life. Hell, we cultivate it. Each and every day of our lives, we water this prized fruit with our tears and our pain. It even receives nourishment from our joys and our happiness. It is not picky----"

"Let's talk about something else," I quickly interrupted.

The probation officer smiled. The glow was dim. "Hear you're a pretty good boxer."

I was startled. "How did you hear about that?"

"At no point since you left town have you been out of my reach, so don't be surprised. In the times ahead, there will be a great number of things that will surprise you, but the fact that I have my resources should not be one of them." He held out his hand. "Ever seen a ring like this before?"

Immediately, I knew I had but I couldn't remember who was wearing it. I looked even more closely at the thin gold ring with the X on it. A single diamond rested in the exact center of the X. Where had I seen a ring like this before? Then it hit me. The Elegant Man!

"So, that's who told you about my boxing? Where do you know him from?"

The probation officer slipped the ring from his finger, ignoring my question. "Give me your hand." The ring fit perfectly. "Now, you're one of us."

"And what is that?"

"A member of The Talented Xth."

"But I don't know what this Talented Xth thing is all about………or who is in it."

"Have no fear. One day you will know everything, and you will lead the group to glory."

"What!!"

"Yes, you," he said sternly. "You will lead The Talented Xth to the ultimate triumph."

I felt choked up. I was also frightened. "But, what must I do?"

"Many great things," he sobbed through tears, "many great things."

"But what if I can't do it. What if I fail?" I shrugged. "Why me?"

"Aren't you tired of asking, why you? As for your other concerns, you can't fail." His voice was as firm as steel. "You won't fail."

"Can I at least know what The Talented Xth is?"

"The Talented Xth, for your information, is people like me, you, and the elegant man."

"*Gays!?*"

"Who else?" His voice turned brassy, and his words sounded like notes from Gabriel's trumpet.

"One day we will rule this country. One day it will be one of our own that will sit in the seat of power, and we will severely punished all those who have openly discriminated against us because of who we are. Then we establish equality for everyone. The Talented Xth will, one day, take over this country in a bloodless revolution, and will bring forth a dynasty that will reign for a thousand years."

"And you actually think this can be done here---in America?" I gasped in disbelief at the stupendous spectacle the probation officer had hatched in his head.

"It can and will be done." He winked slyly at me. "In fact, even now as we speak, it is being done. Members of The Talented Xth are everywhere; lawyers, doctors, politicians. We are not absent in any field."

"Then what the fuck you need me for?"

The probation man grabbed my hand, kissing it respectfully. "You will conquer the world for us."

I buried my head in my hands. "What must I do?"

"Nothing other than what you have already planned to do which is to be the heavyweight champion of the world. Can you do that?"

"Yeah, that's easy," I whispered confidently, "I can do that." A surge of relief flooded my body, hoping this would be all that was required of me. That belief, however, was very short-lived.

"But that's only the beginning. You have promised yourself that you will ultimately win the championship belt, haven't you?"

"Yeah."

"Now, I want you to promise me something."

"What?" My voice was almost unheard.

"Promise me and The Talented Xth that on the night that you win the heavyweight crown and receive the belt that you will renounce it, and announce that you are gay."

"What?! Are you out of your motherfucking mind?"

"That's right," he barked sternly. "That's what I want you to promise me. That simple rejection and announcement will send shock waves throughout the entire world. It would rock this country to its core because it will strike at the heart of their steadfast belief in virile masculinity, and totally dismantle their heroic image of the warrior-king. It would rub their noses in shit to know that the man they have just declared the toughest man on the planet is a sissy. Trust me, nothing else in the world would hurt them as much or as thoroughly." The probation officer paused. "Will you do it?

I couldn't think.

"Promise me."

I wouldn't speak.

"Promise me!"

I could scarcely hear.

"Promise me!!" He commanded me.

"Okay, okay. On the night they declare me the heavyweight champion of the world is the night I will declare that I am a punk."

The probation officer felt back against the pillow. "And, then lead The Talented Xth on to glory?"

"Yes," I muttered, "I'll do it."

"Thank you," he cried aloud.

Then he died.

The   torch   had   been   passed.

BOOK TWO

1

No more Mister Nice Guy!
One of the most common frustrations of my current life was that the best part of it was left behind in the fog of the recent past. What I now experienced more and most of all was the diminished ardor with which I viewed everything around me. Case in point: Nothing mattered.

The rent in my family life was far from normal, and whenever I mentally addressed the relationship between me and my son, I acknowledged that his infantile fury was directly due to his hatred of me. Fuck the little bastard.

If it wasn't for the pretty girl, I would drop his tiny ass off on a church doorstep with a note telling them not to waste any time trying to locate the parents because the boy was unwanted. Still, despite this total lack of domestic tranquility at home, I continued to love the pretty girl. I felt like a sucker for her, and this I didn't quite understand since I spent as much time with my lover as I did her. I could easily walk away. I owed the bitch nothing.

And if that wasn't enough, much of what pumped new life into my anxiety was anchored to the demands of The Talented Xth who sorely needed a poster-boy. I politely assured them that I was not the one. I was what I was, and I was not threatened enough by it, or obsessed enough with it to become a flag-bearer for the cause of it.

On scale, any discrimination that befell me due to my being gay would still be smaller than the discrimination that would be meted out to me because I was black. At least, I had, thus far, done a spectacular job of hiding my gayness although there was nothing I could do to disguise that I was a nigger. I saw little need in adding insult to injury, especially since I was not a glutton for being shit upon.

One other thing. When I got right down to it, what I discovered was that I didn't need The Talented Xth. No fucking way. And I was going to get tough. Hell, I was rich, and that alone gave me the right not to be fucked with.

I phoned the elegant man.

"Guess what?" I half-shouted into the phone, "Since you have been such a good, ol' errand boy for our friends, run and tell this. Tell them I don't want to play with them anymore. Better yet, tell them that I'm getting ready to go on a trip."

"On a trip, huh?" The elegant man slurred into the phone. "You want to go on a trip, do you, you hard-headed bastard?"

"That's right, I'll go on a trip so far that even you guys couldn't find me. How do you like that," I taunted.

He grunted, "Speaking of trips, I've got one for you."

The next day I was drafted into the Army.

The low down, dirty bastards.

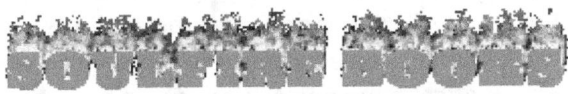

Early on, there was a real fear about being in the Army, and that was mainly because I had never been in an environment where authority went unchallenged. I knew nothing of servile obedience. Even Mother. who had ruled an empire of her own, and had doled out punishment with an iron fist, had urged and encouraged me and my brother to stand firm on our principles, whatever they were, and I had gotten so good at it that is was second nature to me.

I racked my brain for a compromise, some common ground between what I wanted to do and what they wanted me to do, but I discovered none. After a while, I grew tired of trying to come up with something, and I reached a turning point in my life. Well, to be completely candid, it was not, by any stretch of the imagination, a true turning point. What is was, more essentially, was a flying-by-the-seat-of-my-pants, going-right-down—the-middle—of-the-same-road I'd always travelled sort of thing. Fuck conformity. Fuck the military.

I completed basic training, finishing at the very bottom, and was censured severely by my superiors for achieving the lowest possible grades in all my classes.

"You are not fit for any branch of the U.S. Military. You are a complete disgrace to American soldiers everywhere, and you have degraded yourself. You are a snail," the drill sergeant barked. "Do you know what I'd like to do with you?"

I know he didn't really expect an answer, so I offered none. I occupied myself by gazing casually around the office, making amused faces at the family portraits on the big, oak desk.

This enraged him. "You are not at ease, soldier, and I fully expect you to meet my gaze when I'm speaking to you whether you like it or not."

I admit he was quite intimidating.

"I could kill you right now, and guess what, not a word of it would be made public. You'd just be a dead nobody. We're the United States Army, you low down piece of shit. Now, get the fuck out of my office."

I didn't bulge.

"Go on," he yelled, "get out of my breathing space."

I still didn't move.

"Now, you're really going to get it." He was screaming wildly as he raced around the desk, and stood over me with his nose touching mine. "What the fuck is your problem, maggot? Why aren't you long gone?"

"You never gave me permission, sir, to be at ease."

He snarled. "You dumb bastard, you sure picked a fine time to commence conducting your sorry ass like a member of the greatest fighting force in the world, but I'm going to tell you something for your own personal safety. Get the fuck out!"

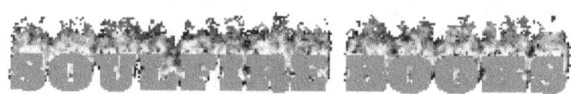

The jungle was hot even when dark. My battalion crept quietly along the eastern perimeter of a deserted enemy encampment. At our backs was a more heavily armed backup unit, and even farther afield was a third patrol squadron.

We moved much like shadows, avoiding the reflection of the moon, each man subconsciously muttering his command orders over and over again in his skull, not wanting to make a mistake, not wanting to die.

As part of the lead-off team, I found myself crawling slowly ahead, carefully picking apart the darkness. Suddenly, upon entering the compound, our commanding officer stopped, moved closer to a charred section of the camp, and whispered into his walkie-talkie, confirming position.

Like professional burglars, we went about our task. I found myself in lockstep with three other soldiers rounding our way to the back door of a very small bamboo hut. I caught an extremely quick movement out of the corner of my eye, but before I could recognize it, the man in front of me was spinning backwards wildly, trying to place his legs squarely under his body. He hit the ground like a rotting tree, and without any further fanfare, he was dead. Then so were the other two soldiers. I hit the ground, terrified, squeezing off round after round into men who came out of nowhere, shooting back.

Within minutes, close to everyone in my battalion had been killed. Behind me, savage fighting continued non-stop, and it was this flurry of activity that drew them away from where I was as I lie trembling on the ground at the bloody boots of one of the enemy soldiers who was firing a single shot from a service revolver into the heads of the fallen and the wounded. They were taking no prisoners.

Too my immediate left, I heard the muffled sobs of someone else who was still alive. In my panic, I spoke too loudly. "Quiet!" I hissed, "Or they'll hear you and come back." Inside my head, I was trying to adjust logic and instinct and anything else I may have forgotten that might help get me out of this situation alive. In a rush of clarity, it dawned on me that what I needed less than anything else in the world was a wounded comrade to care for or about. I glanced over at the still alive soldier, slumped painfully over his rifle, exhaustion and defeat visibly sketched across his face, and with a sudden grim ferocity, I yanked my combat knife from my belt. I rolled backwards, and after two brutal thrusts, he was dead. As I grabbed his gear, I noticed I was shaking so badly that my teeth shook. I checked his weapon and mine, reloading both. It was time for me to move out.

I was nervous, feeling that without a plan, it would be best to just stay put and to pray that reinforcements would soon arrive, but I didn't feel welcome among the dead, so I set out. I unsuccessfully tried to unscramble the tension in my brain, and as I oozed into the thickness of the jungle, I could actually feel death, hearing its babble over and above the other noises of the night. Fear, intense and real, nudged me in one direction, then another so without looking up or knowing my exact position, I exchanged the notion of being extremely cautious for being extremely fast. At the moment, running seemed completely valid.

On the whole, my first hour in the jungle had gone by quickly, and when I stopped to rest, it was not simply to catch my breath, it was too celebrate. So far. So good. Somewhere along the way, my face must have gotten cut because when I touched my cheek, my fingers were warmed by blood. I didn't overly concern myself with it because under the circumstances, bleeding was a bonus.

I started moving again, and though I travelled in the same direction, I noticed that I appeared to be moving upward, steadily, but unperceptively climbing, until, at length, I came to a grassy knoll barely wide enough for me to stand in. It was a look-out post, but it did me little good with darkness caked up in such abundance upon the night.

Squinting in the dim glow of the moon, I crawled to the far end of the slope, and looked over, finding there was a second post directly below it. If I chose, I could drop down to the ledge below, but what then?

In a very patient way, I stood still, absolutely alert, turning slowly and pulling the trigger. My gun spat fire, and although the stink of gunpowder was almost overwhelming, two of the enemy hit the earth. Farther off to my right, I sensed the same thing that had warned me of the presence of the two dead men. I lit up the area with crackling gunfire, acutely aware that I had not missed.

Following a lapse of about five seconds, I let out the explosive air swelling up inside me. I had not even known that I was holding my breath, but when I released the air, it buzzed across my tongue in a heated rush, making me dizzy.

I backed up a few paces and understood that now was a great opportunity to start running. After a long time, I began to feel a bit lightheaded and realized that I couldn't see too well. I also noticed that I was running slowly; to slow, now walking. Something was reducing my odds of survival. I was facing a dilemma of some sort, and it was spinning things around, turning them topsy-turvy; upside down. I smashed into a tree, bounced off, and then noticed that while everything outside was still contemptuously dark, everything inside my head was alive with bright fire.

I clawed at my ears to stop the deafening noise thundering between them. A rivulet of blood flowed freely down the length of my right arm.

"Oh my God!" I cried out. I had been hit.

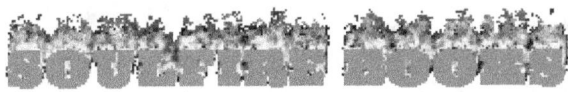

I was coming out of the haze slowly. I knew I should be relieved even though I had no physical forecast of where I would be taken next, or what would happen to me once there. I merely felt as though I had been suspended in a liquid canister where everything had been embellished by a ridiculous slowness.

Another thing I noticed was that my eyes were turned on low, and I was repeatedly blinking them, attempting to adjust them to the proper frequency so I could pick up the meaning behind the frantic actions of the people nearest me.

At the end of another sixty seconds, my eyes took in more. Their reception was rapidly improving. I looked around quickly, panning my eyes from one side of my throbbing head to the other.

Then voices!

Until now, it hadn't dawned on me that prior to that exact moment, my sense of hearing had been cut off. Now, someone had cut it back on, and the volume was much too loud. I screwed up my face to shut off a portion of the noise, especially the......Wait, that was my favorite song. I just had never heard it playing that loudly before.

I understood now. This was death, allowing me the proverbial flashback where my life flashed before my very eyes. WoW! The images of my brother, the pretty girl, my mannish-assed boy were all so perfect, so realistically clear, but where was Mama?

I smiled. The Other Woman had just come into the picture. She reminded me so much of Mother. I wished she would kiss me goodbye.

Oh no, here comes that mannish-assed son of mine. What's that in his hand?........Oh, a little, plastic baseball bat. How fucking cute, I thought even though I had already had this nigger pegged for the chain-gang instead of in the major leagues. Hey, what's that lil' nigger getting ready to do?.......Hit me?.......Damn, sho' is.........Look at his bad ass raising the bat high in the air over his head.......That nigger is really going to hit me.

95

"Drop it!" I screamed and the words came out loud. The little nigger stopped dead in his tracks. My brother and the Other Woman hugged each other happily. The pretty girl cried.

"Welcome back," the doctor said as the nurses clapped their hands.

"You're one tough cookie."

I turned towards the voice. It was the mean ol' Army man. I almost passed out when I saw him. He laughed, and I laughed back so hard that it hurt, but damn, it felt great. That must have been some coma I had been in. The calendar said June. I remembered February. I laughed some more. The enemy hadn't gotten me at all.

Life was good.

It was a very dangerous decision, and to this day, I can't perceive why I was so absorbed in wanting to become a war hero. Maybe I felt I owed the military something. Oftentimes, wounded men frequently developed an emotional bond with the doctors and nurses who had saved their lives, and I could understand that, but why did I carry around this asinine gratitude to the military when all they had done was to expose me to situations that could get me killed.

Maybe that was it. Maybe I wanted to die, or maybe it was just that I only wanted to be as far away from The Talented Xth as possible. Anyway, I turned down the chance to return to civilian life by way of a medical discharge. Instead, I opted to complete my tour of duty. And then I reared up for another tour.

I don't think it was by chance that it happened. These things never do. I had just blazed a blistering firefight with the enemy to save the lives of my commander and two subordinates who served under him. I was lauded and applauded from every quarter for my heroics, and awarded another medal as if I needed more.

After the tiring rounds of interviews with both national and foreign correspondents, I arrived back at base. I had mail. The manila envelope read: <u>Photos enclosed.</u>

I'm glad I sat down.

I half-finished the beer, and ripped the top off of the unaddressed envelope, leaving an ugly gash. I reached and dug out the photos. I jolted upright. Someone was playing a cruel joke on me. They had to be because I was sure he photos were a hoax. Either that or the lights in the barracks were extremely poor.

I shifted the glossy prints this way and that, trying to jiggle the images, to somehow juggle them off the photo, but they wouldn't vanish. They refused to disappear, and they were vivid. And my eyes were not fooling me.

The pretty girl and my brother had gotten married!

It was 72 hours before the mean ol' Army man found me, but by then I was drunken beyond belief. The dingy bar was as way out as one could possibly be without falling off the face of the earth. Yet, he found me. Normally, I would have been impressed. Not tonight.

"Let me assure you that I don't come as an emissary of the US government," I was informed.

"Big deal." I snickered. "Why come at all. I like drinking alone."

"This should come as no surprise to you, but I know of your family problems." He tapped his fingers on the bar, and before I could respond, the bartender had refilled my glass. "Cheers," he grunted impartially. "What I am dying to tell you will both shock and amaze you, I guarantee you that. Are you game?"

I had never seen the Army man so civilian. He appeared, for the first time, ordinarily human. I admit I was drunkenly intrigued. This was so far removed from his well-earned reputation as a no-nonsense, strictly by the books military man.

Of course, I still had suspicions that I couldn't verify, but these only added to the state of drunken allure. I could always take precautions although in this state of intoxication, I had no idea what they were.

"Interested?"

"What's the catch?" I asked.

Finally, a smile creased his face as he dug into the inside pocket of his jacket. "Open your hand."

He allowed me a second to focus.

"Ever see one of those before?"

"*You too*?!" I couldn't hide my surprise. Just as soon as the object touched my hand, I almost dropped it. "Oh, no."

"Surprised?" He plucked the small, gold ring from my outstretched hand. "Or are you shocked?"

"What do you guys want?" I moaned. "Don't you ever get tired or go away?"

"Go away?" he rasped darkly. "Never. Not as long as people like us," he lowered his voice to a faint trace of a careless whisper, "are treated like lepers."

"I can't believe that you, of all people, buy that bullshit. I can almost accept the whining of most of them, but you should know better than anyone in the whole fucking country because your ass is smack dab in the middle of the military which means you know good and damn well what they will do, without a lick of remorse, if a bunch of sissies started talking some bullshit about taking over."

"You overlook the obvious," the Army man cracked. "This is not about the freedom to flaunt our sexual preference, you dumb jock. It's about being free from persecution."

"I wouldn't give a damn if it was about having an orgy on the White House lawn-------fuck you." I looked around for the waiter.

"Forget another drink. Listen. We-----."

I needed a drink bad. "Waiter!"

The Army man scowled. "It should be easier now to announce you're gay since you no longer have a girlfriend."

I was rattled by that last remark. "Don't tell me that you bastards had something to do with that? Please don't tell me that you guys were responsible for my brother fucking my woman?"

"Trust me," the Army man said, "but it was bound to happen because any relationship you have with women is doomed because you enjoy men as much, if not more, that you do women." He snickered. "Have you forget the obvious?"

I couldn't gather my wits together quick enough to respond, so I swirled my beer around in its glass, and watched the foam go round in circles.

"I am not ashamed to tell you," the Army man said, "to stop being delusional because you are just as gay as the rest of us, and it is only a matter of time before someone sniffs you out."

"So what do you want me to do, beat them to the punch and out myself. Is that what you want?'

The Army man chuckled. "That's not it at all. We're on a mission."

I laughed. "I'm rich, bitch," I chanted close to his ear. "I got enough cash to pay for all the sex I'll ever need."

"You think it will be that easy."

99

I laughed loudly. "With money, what isn't?"

To my utter dismay, the very next morning, I learned that money wasn't easy to keep. The pretty girl was suing me. In addition to demanding palimony and child support, I was notified by a threatening letter that the IRS had placed liens on the property that the probation officer had left me. Furthermore, a freeze was put on all monetary assets because it was believed that he may not have been of sound mind when making out his will. Worse yet, a long-lost love child popped up to question the legality of the whole shebang insisting that she alone was most entitled to her daddy's money.

Even my brother joined the charade. In an insurmountable act of stupidity, he informed the Internal Revenue Service of everything there was to know about the proceeds from the sale of the grocery store and the home Mother had got by way of her trickery on the preacher-man. Anyway, since I had benefitted greatly from the sale of the said properties and the income generated from the aforementioned sales, it was deduced that I owed more than a quarter million dollars in unpaid taxes.

I was crushed. And to demonstrate that they were not only arrogant, but also very serious, the IRS bastards gave me a lousy three days in which to surrender my brand new fire-engine red sports car. The gall of those motherfuckers!

I would pull a few strings, and then sit back to see if I had any friends.

3

The little money I had was now gone which meant, among other things, that I couldn't pay for the meal I had just consumed. I looked at the restaurant's owner, and although, from all appearances, he seemed to be a nice fellow, he probably wouldn't be too cheerful if he knew I was planning to skip out on him without paying.

The food had revived my senses, previously dulled by the hunger of not haven eaten for days, and feeling somewhat emboldened, I carefully measured the distance that stood between me and the front door. I had to get a grip on myself.

The reality of capture and jail forced me to consider other options, but I didn't have any. Where did I go now that I'd gone too far? It's always one thing to get yourself into a fiasco, but quite another to get yourself out of it. I remembered that piece of conventional wisdom early enough now that my belly was full. An hour ago, though, the thought of not doing it was the over-riding consideration in my life.

There was no time for regrets now, and I could no longer sit perched over an empty dinner plate.

"More tea, please," I begged the fat, double-chinned waitress. At least, I wouldn't have to worry about this bitch giving hot pursuit since it was evident from her run-over shoes that walking was still an issue for her obese ass.

At any rate, she wasn't the problem. The owner was. I cast a worried glance in his direction and he waved. I returned the gesture while patting my stomach lovingly as if to suggest how fantastic the meal truly had been. I swear that he looked at the cash register in a way that suggestively implied that since I had eaten that the cash was now ready to eat, to be filled with what I owed for the meal.

I looked behind me. The back of the restaurant was deserted except for a worker who was busy doing some empty tables and refilling the salt and pepper shakers. Oddly, there were no back or side door exit.

Slowly, I eased up from the table, scooting the chair back soundlessly. Cautiously, I headed for the entrance. No one noticed, and I was elated. The joy soon died.

"Stop him! Stop him!" It was the owner. "He hasn't paid up."

The big, black chef made a move for me, but he was much too slow. I whirled under his beefy arms and rushed towards the beckoning doorway. Soon, my path was blocked by a pair of pot-scrubbers. I easily dispatched both of them before leaping across a stainless steel prep table. The door was to my immediate right. Two more workers poured in from the left and a woman with a broom emerged from an office near the exit. She swung the broom, but in one quick move, I had wrenched it from her hand. I lashed out at the duo on my left, cracking one solidly beneath his ear. He yelped in pain. The other lost his appetite to fight, but by now, the owner had raced out, and I knew he had called the police.

I slammed through the door.

At the dark end of a dead-end street, I heard several angry voices coming towards me. I quickly saw that I had no place to run, so quite naturally, I searched for a place to hide. I was almost crazy with panic as I yanked the lid off the top of a dumpster and dived inside.

I was busted! I braced myself for the beating I assumed would accompany my arrest, but when the officers lifted the lid of the garbage can, they erupted into uncontrollable laughter.

One spoke up. "Don't you have better sense than to run down a dead-end street when you're trying to elude capture, Mr. War Hero?"

My blood ran cold. War Hero? How did they know that unless........

"Relax, pretty boy," the other cop said, "we are not here to arrest you. We're here to rescue you."

"Does that mean The Talented----"

"Sshh, don't mention that name. Plus, we better get moving." The speaker looked at me. "Let's go."

102

I took one step towards the police car, then executed a move like Barry Sanders, faking the short officer out as he opened the door for me. I ran into the light at the other end of the avenue. Fuck The Talented Xth.

The stale bread was helping. For a while, the first few slices were hard to get down my throat as the dry, crumpled morsels got trapped in my cheeks, clinging to my mouth like silly putty.

The other bum had his back slightly to me, looking vacantly off into the distance, but I could still hear him smacking loudly as he chewed contentedly.

"The trick,' he told me in the voice of an expert, "is to trap spit in the hollow of yo' tongue, and let the bread soak for a second or two before swallowing" He had a wry smile on his face. "Spit sorta softens the bread and the one thing dry bread needs is a lot of moisture." He then dabbed his mouth daintily with the dirty sleeve of his smelly sweater, and afterwards carefully picked the sleeve clean of any crumbs trapped there. These small bits, he redeposited in his mouth. "Waste not, want not," he preached.

The other bum rummaged through the garbage can until he found two more soda cans. "Ah," he exclaimed, "this just might do it." He emptied the remaining contents of the cans into a clear container he had. It was only one third full. "Damn, wasn't but a corner in that can there. We gonna be needing mo' than what we already got if both of us gonna get a good swig out of it." In a short time, he found three more soda cans and an orange juice container. "That should just about do it, my man" he said, pouring the liquids into the clear container. When he passed me the container, he looked at me quizzically.

"What's wrong?" I asked.

"It's better if you hold yo' nose when you drink it the first time or two until you get used to the smell, you know."

"What, it stinks?"

"Naw, my man, it don't stank. It's just that all those flavors be in there, you dig. It's strong, that"s all, but it don't stank."

I held my nose and gulped. It was better than dying of thirst. "Where do we go to wash our faces?" My face felt like someone had been wearing it, and I had a new sore inside my mouth that I wanted to check out. "I need to get to a mirror bad."

"Yeah, my man, you still pretty. You gonna have to take my word for it 'cause we ain't got no time for that shit."

"Why?"

"Food."

"But we just ate."

"I know that, but out here on the bricks, it ain't never too early to start worrying 'bout where yo' next meal coming from." The other bum was serious. "You see, my man, there is thangs out here on the bricks that you ain't never pay attention to when you had money in yo' pockets. When you broker than a motherfucker, it's like life been using trick mirrors on yo' ass, be showing shit that ain't there, you dig, so you gots to be suspicious 'bout everythang."

"Thanks," I said, "I'll remember that."

"Ain't no problem, my man, you dig? You my main man so I gotta school you good. Gonna teach you a lot of shit."

His concern seemed authentic enough. If he felt it was his duty to keep me safe out here in the streets, then I was okay with it, but there was one thing.

"I don't know why I'm telling you this," I began, "but I'm gay." I paused. "I mean, if it's going to cause some kind of problem, I'll go my way. I-I just wanted to be straight with you."

"Straight!?" he laughed, "how a punk ever gonna be straight with anybody. You ain't even being straight with the Lord who made you. He created you a man, and you down heah pretending you a woman." He started crossing the street, stopping in the middle. "Down there," he pointed, "about three blocks 'round that corner is where yo' kind hangs out."

With a sweeping nod of his head, he ran off. I watched him go, not knowing why since he meant absolutely nothing to me although if I was to survive as a homeless vagabond, I certainly could have profited from his wide range of survival skills. I shrugged. Shit, practically everything I now knew, I had learned on-the-fly, by trial and error, so learning to fend for myself would be no different,

It seemed like I had walked for more than three blocks when the specter of how I must have actually looked really shook me. I had only stolen a quick peek at myself in the unflattering reflection of a picture window. Add smell to that image and I could clearly understand why people crossed the street to avoid me. I peered into another window. The reflection was simply a second opinion of the earlier one. I looked horrible.

I smeared a hopelessly radiant smile on my face in a fruitless effort to prove I was still human, and that despite all the wretched shit that had befallen me, life was still good. With a grand flourish. I stood erect, forcing my carriage into a more regal posture. I lifted my head. I looked up. I saw them!

And they were gorgeous!

These, technically speaking, were not 'faggies' these were upper level drag queens, as close to womanly perfection as one could possibly get without going under the knife. There was nothing plain or ordinary about any of them. Each one was exquisite. And no one, and I mean no one, could refute their beauty.

I grew ashamed of myself, nervous that I had to walk past them. What if they smelled me? What would they think of me in my flimsy coat and knocking knees? Would any one of them make me out to be what I was.........one of them? In my condition, I would think not.

Just the same, I crossed the street, and with heavy traffic between us, I let my roaming eyes sweep jealously over them. From what I could tell, the building was some sort of landmark too them, an all-purpose gathering place. By day, a quaint, little gay bar. At night, a hell-on-wheels cabaret.

I was certain that in my present condition, no one would permit me inside, but still I waved happily and wildly at them, an expansive around-the-clock gesture. They took one look and exploded into spasms of girlish giggles. Very seldom had any of them seen someone as hideous so close to their sinfully pretty place.

For the first time in my life, I wished I had one of Mother's dresses, and as an afterthought, a pair of those delicious red, spike-heeled shoes. Suddenly, I felt eerie, standing there fantasizing that it was me that all the well-to-do men in their fancy cars were riding around looking for instead of one of those hussies.

"Hey you!" The voice was icy.

"Me?" I pointed at myself, looking around.

"Yes, you." The man hollered from the window of his long, black Bentley. "I'm talking to you."

Oh no, I told myself. That stud is actually speaking to me, wanting me instead of one of those dolled-up bitches. Wow, that's what my fantasy was all about. He wants ME!

"Come here." His voice was sexy, deep.

I dashed out in the street, still dazed. He wanted me. I stuck out my tongue at the jealous Jezebels waiting from across the street.

"Yes," I purred anxiously as I reached the vehicle. "What may I do for you?"

"Wash my car! Get in."

I was shattered, but I got into the car anyway. At least, those heifers across the street would never know. For all they knew..........

What a ruined fantasy. He had ruined my daydream for this, but at least washing the car would earn me some money for food, so when we pulled up in front of his spacious home, I was relieved to know that I wouldn't starve tomorrow.

"How about a beer, buddy." It was the white man.

"That sounds okay with me," I responded in my best buddy-buddy tone, "but even more than a beer, what I'd like would be to use your bathroom to clean up a bit."

"No problem, buddy. You can take a hot shower if you want to, and still have that cold brewski. I'm kind of celebrating since the wife is out of town and will be gone for a few days." He merrily jumped in the air and clicked his heels together like he was a lucky leprechaun. "And when the cat's away, the mice will play."

"Is that what you were doing over there on the street where those he/she people be?"

He laughed easily, unembarrassed. "Oh that," he shrugged, "was supposed to have been the start of my celebration, but I chickened out at the last possible second. I was afraid of what it might look like picking one of them up. You know, what if someone recognized me, so I ended up with you." He laughed heartily. "Instead of getting my dick sucked, I'm getting my car washed. No offense," he joked, "but I forfeited a chance to get my balls cleaned for the chance to get my wheels cleaned. Some exchange, huh?"

I was no longer paying attention. I was too busy pondering possibilities. "Did you say you wife was gone?"

"She has probably crossed three states by now," he mused.

"Could you show me to the bathroom? Please?"

Prior to the shower, we chatted some and down two beers apiece while I ravenously devoured three slabs of pepperoni pizza. Afterwards, I hurried off to the bathroom. I stripped down, adjusted the water, and stepped under a luxurious cascade on invigoratingly warm water which came out in a delightful spray. How marvelous! The water tickled me, and made me feel alive, bubbly. Slowly, I healed inside as the heat of the sparkling water kissed my tired body and the warmth of the cold beer heated up my soul.

While toweling off, the first wave of apprehension rose up from the passageway of my bowels, but I ignored it.

"You alright in there, buddy?"

"I'm fine," I answered, "be out in few. Can I borrow a razor?"

"In the cabinet, top shelf, left."

Already, I was breathing excitedly, anticipation mounting like crazy. The razor buzzed across my face, mowing down the stubble on and under my chin, and for the occasion, I get rid of my pencil-thin moustache.

Now, came the hard part. Apprehension once more ramping up to subhuman levels as I looked quickly down the hallway to the master bedroom. Quite appropriately, a thousand and one what ifs popped up poking me in the gut, but I knew well in advance what to expect if I succeeded and what to suspect if I didn't.

The die was cast.

Too far gone to turn back now, I dashed into the bedroom, and there at the end of a king-sized bed was the closet. I snatched open the white, wooden, sliding doors and peeked in. My head reeled as I peeked over the articles of clothing until i spotted what I wanted. Now----would it fit?

I held the piece up to my own body, eyeing it for size. Perfect. Then I dropped down on my knees to rummage among the shoe boxes.

Voila!

Next stop: the dresser. By now, the blood was pumping through my veins so hard they thumped, but I was committed, and it was easier now to complete the mission than to abandon it. I ran my hands through all the expensive trinkets in the drawer, making careful choices.

Now, the accessories. Again, I was extremely particular with what I selected. My hands trembled violently each time I fingered a piece of the expensive jewelry, I was virtually hypnotized by the cut, color, and clarity of the dazzling objects, but after carefully examining everything, I chose.

Within a few more minutes, I had accomplished my objective. I looked at myself curiously and smiled. As a clincher, I pulled on a pair of long, black silk gloves, and stared into the mirror again. I was red-hot!

When I reentered the living room, Buddy-Buddy's mouth flew wide open, his jaw dropping to the floor. He was stunned beyond belief. This time when he tried to get his mouth working, he was able to mumble incoherently, but there was still nothing that could be done about the way his eye bulged out of their sockets. They had been arrested by astonishment.

"See anything you like, big boy," I purred sexily.

"Yes, yes, yes," he echoed helplessly.

"Then come to Mama."

He was on his knees in a flash. He crawled to me like a baby.

The Sunday morning sun filtered brilliantly through the parted bedroom curtains, falling across the silk sheets like a jeweled dagger. On the thickly carpeted floor by the bed were the blond wig, the silk gloves, the tight black dress, and the satin panties. All over his pale, contented body were the traces of the candy red lipstick I had so flawlessly applied. And in his heart was love.

His wife now had serious competition.

I met the slut on Tuesday, and at first, she paid me no nevermind and that was just fine and dandy with me and Buddy-Buddy. For all practical purposes, I was a very young friend of her husbands who would be occupying the guest room for a week or so. No big deal.

I rarely spoke to the bitch outside of the customary greetings of hello and goodbye. Once or twice, we tried our hand at polite dinner conversation, but discovered we had very little in common. After this, she didn't say shit to me. I didn't say shit to her.

During the day when husband and wife were at work, I had the run of the spacious house, but I spent most of my time thinking. Once or twice, I managed to get a tidbit or two of news from home, and I struggled with the info that my brother and the pretty girl were making out okay. Sometimes, I wished I had a way to blackmail their asses, or to coerce either one or the other of them to send me money each month, but I had nothing on them.

It also appeared that they had rushed to have another baby. The pretty girl was pregnant, and they were rapidly expanding the nest even more. From what I had gathered, they wanted four children of their own in addition to my little, mannish-assed son. I never ever wondered how he was doing. Fuck the lil bastard.

The Other Woman, on the other hand, had stopped sleeping around and had gotten saved. She sang in the choir on Sundays, taught home economics at church on Tuesdays, and was in all around training to be a saint. I had no idea how sincere she was about her religious conversion, but I do know how serious men were about her sexual perversions, and I felt that at any given moment, those men who had known her in a strictly biblical sense would start rescue missions to deprogram her.

Like Mother, The Other Woman, had good pussy and the connoisseurs of such didn't take kindly to anyone just barging in and interfering with the mechanics of getting their dicks treated real good. They didn't care if it was the church. As a matter of fact, they would rather lose a bitch to the devil than to Jesus.

I had also heard that the probation officer's illegitimate daughter had sashayed into town, filled with righteous indignation that her daddy did not have a more classic epithet on his tombstone. Hell, I was no poet, so I scribbled 'ONE DAY YOU'LL KNOW WHAT THIS FEELS LIKE!' on a piece of notebook paper and told the engraver to put it on the headstone. Shit, I was moved by it, Plus, you couldn't beat its directness.

I could never get any leads on the elegant man. He was a sneaky motherfucker, and ever since that night when I had busted him in his car kissing that other nigger and playing with his dick, he had started to cover his ass much better, That didn't mean he was slowing up, Not by a long shot. No, not the elegant man. There was probably a thing or two he could have taught Mother, and he wasn't being brash, no doubt, when he had boasted that he had stolen many a man from under the noses of bitches who couldn't duplicate or imitate the many sexual tricks at his disposal.

Just thinking of some of his sexual techniques made my mouth water, but when I recalled that he was one of the evil-doers, I quickly weaned myself off the pleasant memories, but still oftentimes, I would surrender to those flashbacks. Then I would have to change my underpants.

I changed the subject. Damn, I was broke. That was another thing about being broke. Somehow, you never forgot it. Even with hunger, there were things you could do that would make you forget you were hungry, but there ain't a damned thing in the world that will make you forget you're poor. And I was so broke that I couldn't make a down payment on a piece of bubble gum.

I went to church! Damn sure did and sang louder than a motherfucker. That's how good I felt when Buddy-Buddy found me a job. Now, all my troubles were over. Whew!

And good news always equaled good sex, but.........?

It was not quite the bewitching hour, but I felt I had waited long enough. I was tingling with sexual ardor, and I had planned to surprise Buddy-Buddy with the best sex of his life. All I had to do would be to wait until his wife went to sleep.

For the occasion, I had chosen a pair of his wife's most expensive silk panties, and to accent the sheer black undergarments, I pulled on a pair of matching black stockings. I teased the dark wig, and left the guest room. Suddenly, I had to piss, and this is where my best laid plans fall apart at the seams. If only I had held that piss. After all, since a good piss only lasts a few lousy seconds, I neglected to lock the bathroom door, and just as I was standing over the commode, shaking the last drops of piss from my dick, guess who walks in-----the wife!

The sight of me standing there in her 'things' with my thing in my hand must have knocked the sleep from her eyes. She stood perched in the doorway, gazing brazenly, digesting the whole picture. "Are those mine?" She meant the 'things'.

I was afraid to answer.

"And is all of that-----YOURS?!" She meant my thing.

I nodded slowly, and like a trained laboratory pet, my dick rose up
to   greet   her,   stretching

110

through my outstretched fingers, growing to its full magnificence. This impromptu demo impressed her.

"Oh my goodness," she moaned. "Fuck me, you nigger."

I guess the spectacle of her things contrasted against the firmness of my thing went to her head, overwhelming her. Still, she didn't have to be so racist about it, though.

I spun her ass around like a pearl white spinning top, bent her over the sink like a pretzel, and piled her silk gown on her back, and went into her from behind. She loved it. I knew that from the way she rocked and moaned and moaned and rocked, so I put it to her harder. She moaned louder, liking it even more. I was bent over her back, riding her like she was a wild, untamed bronco, and when we hit the zone, I screwed my face up into a twisted ball of contentment, and looked up to let loose a savage groan of completion, but it was then that I became acutely aware of three things. First, I was about to get a nut. Second, the bathroom door was wide open, and third, Buddy-Buddy didn't like what he was seeing.

Essentially, he was steaming hot, furiously red in the face. "Go home to your parents" he screamed at is wife. "You," he angrily pointed at me, "go to the devil."

See there. Now, I was convinced that white folk couldn't or wouldn't, under any circumstances, treat niggers equal to them. I guess that it just wasn't in their nature. Here we were, me and his wife fucking each other to death, doing the same thing at the same time with each other. Yet, he subjects us to different punishments. He tells her to go home, but tells me to go to hell!

I don't care what white people do, they always just gonna get a slap on the wrist, but right then I was in no position to argue, so I snatched my dick out of his wife and grinned dumbly just like someone who had just been caught red-handed. I guess I could kiss that job goodbye.

Undoubtedly, to show that he had a heart, before leaving Buddy-Buddy allowed me to get properly dressed, and to pack a few personal items for my journey. I kept the pantyhose on, and stuffed the wig into a duffel bag along with a red dress and matching heels. I stole his razor.

I swiped a few dollars off the kitchen table as the wife begged Buddy-Buddy to let me fix myself a few peanut butter and jelly sandwiches to put in my stash, but that idea was rejected initially, but I was grudgingly granted permission to make two sandwiches.

I departed the premises with thirty-five dollars and two sandwiches, and I expected no sympathy from the bitches on the block. This was going to be a most interesting day. At the local Five and Dime store, I stole mascara, eyeliner, powder puff, blush and some other petty shit. Then I rushed to the public restroom to do the drag queen equivalent of what Clark Kent did when he dashed into a phone booth-----to transform and to transcend; to become super!

When I alighted from the men's dressing room, decked out in my gear, a store clerk looked at me searchingly, sure that I had made use of the wrong restroom, and that was the mental spark I needed to get my adrenaline juiced up.

At the exit door, a tall, handsome nigger licked his tongue out at me lewdly. I giggled like a school-girl. That nigger there was a pussy-hound if there ever was one, and if I could fool him, then there was nowhere to go but up.

I hailed a taxi, but had only a hint of where to go. "Take me to that hangout place across town where all the drag queens be."

The taxi driver looked me over carefully. "You're not one of them, are you?"

"Yes, I am," I snapped, "and damn proud of it."

"No offense, but you could have fooled me." He was in denial; shocked.

From the back seat of the cab, I peeked out of the window and recognized the old stone building, and as usual the street pulsed with electricity. The entire block shimmied with the festive chaos of a carnival. Businessmen pulled up in their company cars, pulling out seconds later with a mid-day companion. Cops on the take looked the other way.

And the Queen Bees were out in full regalia.

"Stop right here," I ordered the cabbie. "I'll walk the rest of the way." I paid the fare.

I started off down the street deliberately slow, but when the taxi driver cruised past, he blew his horn at me. For me, the honk of that horn was like introductory fanfare, a brassy drumroll that caught everyone's attention. All eyes were on me, and with this type of a head-start, I made the best of the opportunity, snuggling into everyone's line of vision like a gorgeous mirage. Was I real? Was I a vision? At first, no one was sure.

Passers-by honked and whistled. The cop on patrol halted traffic at the intersection just so I could cross the street safely. All the Queen Bees twisted around nervously, taking long looks and then conferring among themselves. I was too close now for any of them to pretend I was a mirage or a vision. That settled, they huddled together like noisy porcupines.

I smiled at their dilemma, but despite my cool exterior I still entertained butterflies in the pit of my belly. Needless to say, it didn't help my stomach any when one of the drag queens, the hugest of the group, approached me. She had taken no more than two or three giant steps before her smile vanished and her cute, little switching walk turned into more of a military goose-step. I tried not to appear frightened.

"Who the fuck are you, and where the hell you come from? The voice was a lot less bright than the clothes. "None of us sent for you. Shit, none of us even know you."

I hissed. "I must have lost my invitation, but the last I heard it's a free country, and one can go wherever one wishes." I rolled my eyes. "You think I need an invitation to that?" I nodded my head at the hang-out spot. "Get real, bitch."

"Oh, so you're a tough broad, huh? Is that what my first impression is supposed to be. Well, let me tell you something, Miss Cheap Perfume, it's not. And it would pay to remember that nothing scares me."

"That's my line," I sneered, "I ain't scared of shit either so that means one of us lying, and since I believe I'm the most fearless bitch on the planet, I'm calling you a liar."

That unnerved the drag queen. She took two steps back, bracing for combat. "Bitch!" she screamed.

A brand new car pulled up to the curb and honked. "Hey you, let's go."

I spun on my heels and left the drag queen standing there, boiling with rage. I was off to an auspicious start.

It was a few days before I went back down to the hang-out spot, and just as soon as I hopped out of the cab, the head Queen Bee came rushing in my direction.

"You ain't nothing but trouble," she howled.

"And good morning to you, too," I calmly responded.

"Fuck the pleasantries," He/She snarled coldly. "We took a vote and we don't want you in."

113

"Splendid, if that's what wet your panties, I'm out. No big deal. I'm flattered that I was even considered, especially when I didn't ask none of you bitches for shit. Vote?! Y'all hoes make my dick draw up."

"I thought you had gotten my number the last time we had our lil, street corner conference?"

I moved into position to unleash a barrage of punches. "Your number don't mean shit to me."

The slight movement did not go undetected. He/She was sizing me up. If it came to blows, both of us knew it wouldn't be, by any means, feminine. No wild windmill swinging. No hair pulling. No scratching. None of that catty shit would apply here. It would be strictly blood and broken bones. Two professionals duking it out until one was punched out. We both realized what we were up against with the other, and we stood stock still because any move, however slight, would call forth bloody mayhem. Right at that moment, it was expressly clear to me that I would have to kill if, I myself, was to get out alive.

"*Wait!*"

It was more a command than a plea of any sort, so we both turned to face the voice. He/She's face became livid.

"Haven't you been warned about sticking yo' nose in grown folks' biz'ness?"

"I'm just so tired of you bossing me around all the time telling me what to do. Some of the others are tired also." The voice belonged to a tiny individual dressed in scarlet with matching knee boots.

I exercised my cunning. "I think another vote is in order, but this time the vote is for a new Queen Bee."

"Yea," Tiny shouted. "Let me go tell the others."

And just like that, I was in the running for Queen Bee."

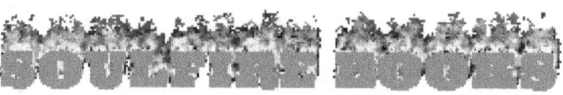

Over the last two weeks, I had been in on a series of the worst shocks of my life. I found that campaigning for office, whether political or homosexual, was more time-consuming than training for a championship fight.

The whole shebang was a patchwork of intrigue, double-crossing, and lying through your teeth, but I learned fast and that was a good omen.

Another even better sign was that most of the queen bees were ready for change. They all had their individual reasons, but it all amounted to the fact that many wanted He/She out and someone else in. The trouble was that He/She had a fairly tight-knit clique of yes-persons who benefitted greatly from being so close to the seat of power, and now they were beginning to feel threatened which translated into a lot of grief for me. They were digging in for a fight.

For some reason of my own, I really didn't feel particularly enthused about getting bogged down into a long, drawn-out power struggle that could fracture the Queen Bees permanently, especially since I wouldn't know how to fix the damage done, but I couldn't concede defeat either.

In any event, I was in for the long haul, come what may. I didn't find myself eager, but if worst came to worst, I couldn't prove to be any more worse a leader than He/She was, but first, I had to get the votes out. The task before me was simple: prevent my adversary from winning.

Since politics was so new to me, I guess that I should have been more careful about unburied skeletons in my closet, especially fresh ones as these seemed to always rattle loudest.

Well, today was the day.

When I entered the great meeting place, I was shouted down with a loud, raucous din of boos. Very spirited.

"Apostate!"

"Back-slider!"

"Two-timer!"

I tried to make sense of it all, but there were so many accusations flying around that it made my head spin. What was happening, I wondered. What was this all about? What did it all mean?

From the look of smug satisfaction of He/She's professionally made-up face, I knew I had located the instigator of this madness, or at least who would be willing to take credit for it. More swearing and curses rang out, filling the great hall with a profane solemnity. Even Tiny, my most trusted supported looked upset. Something big had happened here that had no precedent, and everyone was aware that I somehow had authored it. But what?!

"Tramp?!

"Scavenger!"

More ugly words were hurled from all directions, sapping my morale. I plopped down into my seat, waiting anxiously to hear the serious charges that were being leveled against me. From somewhere in the back of the room, someone with powerful lungs let loose a most deafening high-pitched whistle. Instantly, the place grew silent.

I waited for the ax to fall, and it wasn't long in coming. As soon as He/She rose up to speak in the great meeting place, the whole atmosphere turned oppressive. Even though I couldn't yet decipher the look of unmitigated triumph on his face, the words were unmistakable lucid.

"Oh, Queen Bees," He/She intoned grandly, "we gather here in the refuge of our great meeting place to resolve ourselves of the filth that has entered in upon us. Even now, as I speak, I must be mindful of what I say because in this, our sanctuary, we are obliged to say that which does the least harm. The revered walls of our great meeting place have ears and long will they remember what will be said here and recorded for posterity." He/She looked at me momentarily and then yanked his vision away. His purple-lined eyes fluttered in disgust. He put his hands, with their lacquered nails, upon the sides of his exquisitely-coifed hair as if he had to think something over with himself.

Everyone twitched in the silence, even me.

"Excuse me," He/She apologized, "but I want to be fair. I want to be just. This historic moment is bigger than me, bigger than all of us, bigger than......" He glanced at me. "Anyway," he groaned, "I felt that, well, being the person I am, you know, loving and generous, that I, well, I just had to stand up here and search my heart to make sure that I was doing the right thing by spilling my guts," With a few deft movements of his hands, He/She had managed to draw attention to the fact that tears were streaming from his eyes. "I'm alright, I'm alright," he apologized, "but when our very existence is threatened, and our character assassinated, I, for one, ain't having it."

In the end, what it all came down to was the fact that I had somehow failed to bury my past deep enough, that my past had somehow came back to haunt me, big-time, because once it was ceremoniously disclosed that I had fathered a child, I was booted out as an outcast. Of all the things I was permitted to do with an appendage, my dick, that I didn't truly need, sticking it in a woman was the ultimate no-no. For us, a dick, for all practical purposes, was simply a pisser. You used it only when you had to tinkle. At all other times, it should be tied down and tucked away.

116

Throughout the course of my life, I had heard countless tales from men who spoke of the dangers of letting their dick get them in trouble, but I never thought, for a single second, that this would be one of my woes. But it was, and because of it, I kissed away or more colorfully, pissed away my chances of being Queen. Instead, I ended up getting royally screwed.

Of course, Tiny's contact with me got him suspended from the Queen Bees, so he tagged along with me to the point of no return. In a desperate move to protect ourselves and meager belongings from the elements, we managed to snag a one-bedroom apartment down by the river. Tiny, bless his little heart, worked on an honest job at a construction site. Lord knows, what he did, but I felt so guilty when he came home at night, smelling like a musty old man. We had to do something quick.

Then Tiny got fired! At once, I became very interested in what we were going to do next, but Tiny acted as if we had loads of social security rolling in that would permit us to retire and to live comfortably. I didn't know exactly how to explain our desperate situation to Tiny because he was in denial.

"I got a plan,' was all he would say. "I just need to work out a few kinks."

One day, just after lunch, Tiny came skipping in the apartment, demanding my undivided attention. "I been telling you that I had a plan, remember.   Well,   here   it   is."

I stepped immediately to the other side of the third doorway and glanced at my watch. Had it been thirty minutes already? I checked the apartments once more. Yes, this was the third doorway on the hallway, next to the stairwell. No doubt, this was the spot.

Did Tiny remember to leave the door unlocked like he said he would? I tried the knob. He remembered. The door was open, and I slowly pulled the gun out of my coat. Just feeling the weapon made my body tingle, but I reminded myself that I was not back in a rice paddy in Southeast Asia.

My throat felt dry.

Then I was inside the apartment, my eyes instantly adjusting to the light as I made a quick, thorough sweeping search with them. By the time the startled man realized what was happening, I already knew he was harmless and that there were no weapons close at hand. I visibly relaxed.

Seeing me, Tiny snapped into action. I tossed him the rope, and he bound the man's hands and feet securely. I left him to his work, and occupied myself with ransacking the apartment in search of valuables.

Within minutes, we had his stuffed wallet, his jewelry, and countless other salable items that I jammed into a pillowcase. The man said nothing the whole time. He trembled, watching us.

We darted out of the apartment and dashed down the flight of steps, but just as soon as we got to the bottom of the stairway , I glanced up in time to see the man, hopping out of his doorway. As he got to the top of the stairs, he lost his footing. He began to topple forward, but without the use of his hands to balance himself, he plunged down the stairs. Falling, he made a loud, terrible noise, but Tiny and I both stood at the bottom, transfixed, watching. He hit each step hard, bouncing off and plummeting down to the next one, rolling over and over like a sack of rotten potatoes.

When he crashed onto the landing, he was a mess of spurting blood. He groaned pitifully, looked at us through glazed eyes, and coughed up a glob of phlegm. A couple arrived in the doorway, saw the dead man, saw Tiny, saw me. Saw the sack of stolen goods. Then they looked at one another.

Tiny and I disappeared.

The jailer turned on his heels and left me posted in front of a tottering, tripod camera.

"Hold still," he barked, "and bring that nameplate up closer to your chin….Yeah, stop. That's good. Don't move." The camera exploded in a flash of white light. I blinked my eyes to shut out the blinding light.

"Turn to your right."

Another eye-popping flash.

"Okay, now, turn the other way."

Flash went the camera.

"Now," I was told, "go over to that booth where your friend is and we'll get you fingerprinted."

I shuffled over a few feet to the area where a burly deputy was busy twisting Tiny's fingers into a smear of gooey black ink, and then applying the print onto a white card. I watched vacantly as he did this to all of Tiny's fingers. Satisfied with the results, he handed Tiny a cheap pen and told him to sign his name on the bottom of the card.

Next, it was my time.

This done, both Tiny and I were herded into a square cubicle with all the other misfortunate men who had been arrested and were now being processed into the county jail. The cubicle, although crowded, was particularly quiet. Each man was more or less preoccupied with his own fate.

After being fingerprinted and having mug shots made, I wondered what more there could be to this jailhouse ritual of getting registered into hell on earth. Momentarily, they called my name, along with Tiny's, and a few of the others. We were made to walk in a single file along the right side of a narrow corridor where we were marched to the rear section of a large enclosed area where there were green storage bins filled with standard-issue jailhouse gear.

In each separate bin, there were giant fading letters that denoted size. When the jailer got to me, he went over to the bin marked 2x and tossed me a pair of orange pants and a matching top.

"What size?" The jailer was staring at my feet.

I told him and he dutifully retrieved a pair of used shower shoes from a shelf. Another jailer entered from a side door, his arms loaded with towels, sheets, and a small plastic bags of toilet items. He divided the items into equal piles, a stack for each prisoner.

The first jailer barked orders. "Strip down, take a shower, and change into your jail clothes. Put all your personal things into those boxes. Only thing you can keep is ten dollars in money. Everything else will be stored until you are released or sent to prison."

Even before I left the showers and put on the drab jail gear, I was beginning to feel dehumanized. It was as if I was about to be deprived of any individuality that I might have had, and, of course, I instantly felt robbed of my dignity. Individually dressed, and loaded down with our gear, we were moved through a cold, well-lit tunnel similar to the one we had just left, except this one was not crowded.

Directly in front of us was a bank of phones and after a short, few minutes, the officer had them turned on. "Use the phone if you want to. In about thirty minutes, all of you will be taken upstairs to the cell blocks."

Thirty minutes later, we stepped into an elevator. The jailer punched 2, and when the creaky elevator reached the second floor, the doors rattled apart, opening into a fairly wide corridor. Some names were called, and those inmates disembarked. Tiny and I were not among that group.

We whizzed past the third floor, but on the fourth, a single person got off there. That left only Tiny and me who evidently were going to the maximum security ward which is where those charged with armed robbery and murder, such as me and Tiny, were housed

Two more officers were waiting to escort us to the cellblocks as both of us prayed we wouldn't be separated.

"Put them both in C-6."

By now, we had come to the first sliding gate, and when it opened we went through to the next gate where the officer spoke into a box mounted on the wall. The gate slid open noiselessly, and we were handed over to another guard who produced a giant key and inserted it into a gash in a steel door. The door swung out into a dimly lit corridor.

"All the way to the back," the jailer instructed before slamming the heavy door closed.

I don't know what I was expecting, but this was a lot nicer. I sighed in relief. C-6 was composed of two-man cells, and as soon as Tiny and I got settled in, we hugged each other gratefully. We were glad we had not been separated because it was clear to the two of us that over the long haul, we would need each other for support, and if lonely enough, for love.

At dawn, me and Tiny were roused from sleep by a heavyset jailer who rushed us out of the cellblock without allowing us brush our teeth or to wash our faces. We were on court call, and we had to be on time. Even though, I was new at this, I couldn't imagine a Judge being up this time of morning, no matter how much zeal he had for his job.

All the inmates who were scheduled for Court were fed breakfast in a huge waiting pen, and then one by one we were called out, and allowed to change back into our civilian clothes. After I had changed clothes and had returned to the holding cell, some guy was sitting real close to Tiny. Too close, but from the looks of it, Tiny was enjoying the company.

I shook off the jealousy, and found a place to sit in a far distant corner, but after a while, Tiny noticed that I kept watching him, and reluctantly came over to sit with me.

"He's nice," Tiny offered

"I hope you not planning on setting up house in here and getting cozy with some trifling-assed crook."

Tiny's eyes blazed. "For your information., big sister, I have no intention of getting married in here, but what's wrong with making the best of a bad situation?"

"There's plenty of reasons," I shot back.

"Such as?"

"First of all, you're not supposed to like it in here. This is not a single's bar. This is jail." I turned slightly to the side. "This conversation is finished with."

"It is, is it?"

"Yes ma'am."

"Says who?"

"Says me."

We both laughed.

"Ain't nothing wrong in admitting a little bit of jealousy," Tiny scolded me. "I'm kinda into you like that and I wouldn't want you to shut me for someone else."

"Girl, you a trip."

"But ain't nothing like being a trip with someone you care about."

At around nine o'clock, we were led out of the waiting pen and marched like a detachment of condemned men into a huge, cold Courtroom. We all sat in a gallery to the right side of the Judge's bench, and at precisely or shortly after the hour, the Judge strolled in. Everyone was compelled to stand up as the bailiff mumbled some legal mumbo-jumbo that authorized whatever was going to happen next---to happen.

The proceedings were assembly line precise. Without giving much thought to what he was doing, the Judge either set bail or denied it. He also appointed free lawyers to represent those of us who couldn't afford to hire one.

We made it back to the cellblock just in time for lunch. I was sick to the bottom of my stomach, but knew I had to eat. The Judge had refused to set bail in our case, and I had no idea when the case would be called up for trial, but even then it wasn't like they would be any reasonable likelihood of release. I was absolutely sure of that, and deep down, I was convinced that Tiny knew it as well. We were goners, for sure, but the jailhouse part of doing time was the hardest. You had too much idle time, too many opportunities to think bad thoughts about shit over which you had no control. And most of the shit that would determine how bad your future was going to be would be placed in the hands of a lawyer who had no real interest in you.

I met my court-appointed attorney at three, and once he had completed a quick review of my case, and had culled from me the events that had led to it, he lost not a moment in telling me that "it doesn't look good, doesn't look good at all. Murder," he added, "is not a very good crime to get caught for."

"But I didn't commit a murder."

"That is a point that can be argued, but by your own admission, you did commit the armed robbery. That, by itself, could be as nasty to defend as murder."

"Then, what do you suggest?"

"Give me some time to talk to the county prosecutor to see what his feeling are?"

"What good will that do?"

"Sometimes, much, sometimes nothing." The lawyer shrugged. "There were two of you, right?"

"Yeah, that's right."

"That right there should offer a clue."

I didn't get it.

"Professionally, I can't presume upon you to consider this, but for your own good, it might not be such a bad idea if you admitted to the Court that you were coerced into this crime by your co-defendant."

"You-you want me to put the weight on my friend?"

"Better him than you, but I advise you that I advise you of no such thing, however I'm telling you this. Jail separates friends quicker than a con man separates a fool from his money. I advise you to keep that in mind. This is not The Good Ship Lollipop, my friend. This is the Titanic where you either sink or swim, where it's every man for himself." He peeked at his watch. "Right about now, your co-defendant's lawyer is running this same storyline by him, and one of the two of you is going to bite." The lawyer shrugged again. "Everywhere across the country, the game is played the exact same way."

"Well, you looking at a person who doesn't play by those rules, especially when a close friend is involved."

"Didn't you understand what I said a second ago about friendships and what happens to them in jail?"

I stared at the floor, confused.

The lawyer talked casually. "I know what you're facing, but it's much worse than it appears. Can you imagine waking up every day for the next twenty years with someone telling you what to do, when to do it, and where best to do it. Prison is far worse than jail. Jail wounds you. Prison mutilates you, tearing you up in itty-bitty pieces so tiny that you will never be able to put yourself back together again." He stared at me curiously. "What you have gotten yourself into is no paint-by-number dream. This is a nightmare and prison is as real as hell is hot." He stood to leave. "Have a pleasant evening."

Within two weeks, Tiny had practically taken up with another inmate on the tier. Basically, the only time I got to see him was at court time, or lock-in time for the night. He was forever bringing me books, or stuffing candy under my pillow. Sometimes, he would draw funny cartoon faces and put our names under the looney characters, but he seldom had any real time for me. It was clear what was going on. One day when I walked past the cell where Tiny's new friend slept, a curtain was up and Tiny was inside.

Later, during the four o'clock count, Tiny pranced in having just come from the shower, still dripping wet, a towel around his waist.

"What you gonna do now," I cracked meanly, "Suck every dick in C-6?"

Tiny was surprised by my verbal attack. "It's none of your business what I do. What you need to do is to stop running around playing Mr. Golden Gloves Champ and get some of this free dick. I'm definitely taking advantage of this opportunity. Lonely motherfuckers pamper you real good." He giggled. "I just love it when a nigger calls me by his woman's name. That's the greatest feeling in the world." He moved closer to my bed. "And let me tell you something else. I'm the one with the power. I makes them niggers beg, and they feel good spending money on me. Some of 'em, I simply take the place of their women. Some, I make forget about their women. Others, I become their woman."

Who was I to argue?

In fact, I had no argument because of all the places and spaces on the planet, jail was an exception to every rule imaginable. In jail, you had to truly get in where you fit in since when you under lock and key, there are no identifiable safe havens or neutral zones.

"Just be careful," I admonished Tiny before slipping back into my thoughts, and as usual, the first thing I noticed when I deliberately shut the external world down is how scary it can be inside your mind.

You never truly get used to being in jail. At best, you find a familiar place where the pain threshold is not so unbearably unreasonable and you stay there, And then you learn all of your 'not too's' as soon as possible. You learn not to expect shit. You learn not to get hungry. You learn not to trust your lawyer. You learn not cry.

But you cry just the same.

A few days later Tiny started getting high. Most of the morning, he was careful to avoid me, but when I saw him stumbling over his own feet for no apparent reason, I suspected he was buying someone else's medication.

When I mentioned it, we had a mild argument, but our lines of communications were left open, so I would always have a chance to have my say. And then one day right out of the blue, Tiny developed an annoying cough, and was forever drinking water, complaining of his throat being dry all the time.

"If you admit it or not, Tiny, the only thing making you sick is because you taking all these different kinds of pills that you be buying on the tier. Honey, those pills are colorful and pretty, but they ain't no M&Ms."

"And who asked you for a medical review? Between you mother-henning me, and them stupid niggers out on the tier, it's a fucking wonder I ain't crazy."

"I do what I do out of love. Everybody else out there just want to fuck you."

Sensing my eagerness to argue, Tiny lowered his voice to a whisper. "Let's end this conversation, please." He turned his cheek towards me. "Give me a big, good night kiss, and let's get some sleep ."

The next morning when the doors opened at six, Tiny didn't get up. I didn't disturb him as he had developed the habit of not being "too hungry in the a.m.", and would occasionally skip breakfast. Fasting was not my thing. I ate three meals a day, every day as well as all the 'goodies' Tiny brought to the cell. I ate.

On my way back to the cell, I couldn't help but notice the two or three jailers hovering outside my cell, shooing other inmates off. Of course, my initial reaction was too walk faster, but then I thought that Tiny could handle whatever it was that had drawn them to our cell like flies to a stack of shit. Anyway, it was probably nothing more than a rookie trying to compel Tiny to get up and make the bed up. *But this was Saturday.* I unconsciously began to walk faster, but, for some reason, almost grinding to a complete halt when I saw the resident nurse step out of the cell, shaking her head no

NO!

I started to run, but knew that I couldn't, wouldn't get there in time.

NO!

They brought Tiny out on a stretcher. I looked directly at the head nurse, my eyes asking the question. Her eyes answered, telling me everything I needed to know.

Oh no.

Tiny was dead!

I fainted.

When I regained consciousness, it was the next morning. The medical staff had decided not to risk another suicide, so they had kept me under around-the-clock suicide watch.

At noon, they brought me a fresh tray of French fries and a pair of hot dogs. I merely picked at the fries and ignored the franks. I did, however, down the Kool-Aid.

While examining the ketchup and mustard packets, a jailer from my cell-block approached my room. "Get dressed, attorney visit," he croaked.

I hesitated.

"Now," he commanded.

Upon entering the visiting room, I realized just how pale my attorney actually was. He was purposely ignoring me it seemed as he made a great pretense of hunting for something in his briefcase. He addressed me loosely, spitting my name and good morning out as if speaking too loudly would disrupt his concentration and detract from his paper chase.

"Aha," he whistled, "here it is." He studied the contents of the documents as if he was seeing them for the first time, and when he was certain the wording had changed none, he shoved the document at me. "Sign it!" he ordered.

"Sign it?"

"Yeah, sign it, you know, like writing your name on the dotted line." He pointed. "Right there."

"But what-------?" I cut myself off abruptly. I was frozen. I hadn't noticed it before. The ring. He was one of them.

"What's wrong, Champ?" he grinned, "the cat got your tongue?"

"This paper, what is it?" My voice trembled.

"It's your confession."

"Confession?"

"I wasn't up all night for nothing, putting this together so sign it and this whole ordeal will be over."

"How? What do you mean?"

"Just what I said. It will be over. In your confession, your deceased friend did everything. You were outside and had no idea what was happening inside. When you went in to investigate, your friend, now deceased, handed you a pillowcase with unknown contents, just as the victim tumbled down the stairs."

"But the couple, they saw me."

"Did they see you in the apartment?"

"No."

"Okay, that means you were never in the apartment."

I was beginning to get the picture.

"The victim."

"And where is he?"

"Dead."

"Who else knew?"

"My co-defendant."

"And where is he?"

"May his soul rest in peace," I whispered.

"And all the couple can testify to is what you've confessed to. In light of everything, your good friend is the guilty one, and he is in no position to defend himself from the grave. I know that, you know that, and more importantly, the DA will know it so there is absolutely no way he'll go to Court------."

"H-how you know that he won't want to go to Court?"

"Because, dammit, I've already spoken to him, and if you hurry up and sign, I can hurry up and get it back to him, and they can hurry up and get you out of here."

"Then, what?"

"You go home, Champ. In exchange for your signature, he's willing to dismiss all charges against you."

"May your soul rest in peace, Tiny," I solemnly muttered. "Thanks for giving me back my freedom. I love you." Then I signed my name with a happy flourish.

BOOK THREE

Tiny's death had been a resource that I would not allow to go uncompensated for. Of all the things he had given me, his final gift had proven to be the best, and I promised myself that no matter what, I would not pass on this new lease on life as though it was a trivial offering. What had been given me was no lucky fluke, and I had every intention of now being very sensitive to both my freedom and my life. Starting here and now, I would be a better influence on myself.

This was no laughing matter and while I couldn't or wouldn't endeavor to polish up and spit shine all the embarrassing decadence that tainted my soul, I would permit the most vulgar embellishments to decay via neglect and/or atrophy. I would change myself.

The future held out a good number of exciting possibilities, but any time I made the effort to sort them out, one clearly stood out from the others, and notwithstanding how I shuffled and juggled other probabilities, it beckoned much more radiantly than any of the rest. It demanded investigation, but the risks attendant upon that course of action would not provide me the luxury of turning back to where I was or what I was.

Yet....?

Being in jail had introduced a sort of domestic turbulence in my life that I was not trained to shake. As a result, I was never perfectly safe from the kind of things that could destroy me mentally. I had to make a stand. I had to make a change. I had to. There was no other choice.

At so many times during the day and night, my mind was a sparkling reservoir of sullied images. They all, well, most of them anyway, contained memories of me and Tiny, and I became highly sensitive to them. In my head, I visually witnessed Tiny going through the tedious process of preparing a way for death. All the glaringly covert and overt actions that preceded the actual suicide were there. The letting go of oneself, the constant preoccupation with nothing; the justification of everything by making it a friendly act. Everything that he did now had a name, and none of the good he did for me was commissioned as payment for any debt he felt he owed for getting me in trouble, but rather as bargaining chips for my belated forgiveness for what he would do to himself. Accordingly, he was forgiven.

Now, I also felt haunted by my after-the-fact identification with the wholesale discrimination that hounded gays. In jail, I got a close up view of it as it hunted Tiny day after day, but this was not just a jailhouse phenomenon. It was rampart everywhere. Maybe the Talented Xth was right. Perhaps, gays deserved to be treated as human beings.

Being in jail had really opened my eyes. Discrimination against gays was real, and I remembered what the probation officer had told me about the microcosm and the macrocosm, how the small reflected the large. This provided me the inspiration to look beyond what I had witnessed Tiny go through in jail, and to understand that it happened on a much wider scale throughout the world to countless members of the gay community.

I made a decision, an irrevocable one. I was on the verge of crossing the line in the sand, and I very well knew it when I picked up the phone with both my hands trembling and sweating. I punched in the digits, and when I heard the voice on the other end, I spoke clearly and firmly.

"Yo, elegant man. I'm in."

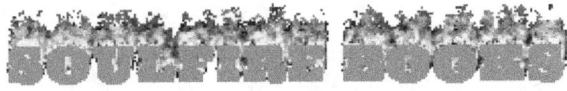

My first months back in the gym were torturous, but slowly I began once more to look like a fighter. Most of my brilliant ring assets I had not lost, but they were buried under years of ring rust. One by one, I restored them.

At first, the elegant man was upset. "You'll never make it back one hundred percent. None of them do, not even the better ones. Why kill yourself with all this unnecessary training? You've been told a thousand time that matches can be arranged------."

"And I have told you that many times plus more that I'm gonna win the belt fair and square. If I gotta give the belt up, at least I want to earn it legally."

"You're a bigger damned fool now than you were when you were young. Who you trying to impress anyhow? You trying to impress that little, pretty girl that your brother stole right from under your red nose?"

I started to protest. He stopped me.

"Don't say shit. Listen! Yeah, that's what you do. Listen. You lost that pretty girl for the same reason you're going to lose in the ring. You can't think worth two cents. You think people and events just gonna hang around and wait the fuck on you. Well, dig this. It don't work like that. It ain't happening, you hear me? It ain't happening, ain't never happened for anyone else, and it certainly not going to happen for a red, snot-nosed punk like you."

I began to pound the heavy bag more savagely, mercilessly punching it until the ceiling rattled. The elegant man wouldn't go away, even though he could see I was deliberately ignoring him. As he continued to talk, my punches became more powerful.

"This game requires guts that you ain't got no more. "You're an over-the-hill punk, and I mean punk in the literal sense. All your affairs in the ring were settled long ago, so don't come dragging your ass back, riding on your old reputation. Nigger, ain't no more glory left for you because your time in the spotlight is gone. Your time is up. Your heart pumps Kool-Aid, I know it and you know it, so let us fix things in the background. Face it, the championship is beyond your reach."

Even after the elegant man was gone, I couldn't stop my hands from hitting the bag. During my entire life, I had never realized anything even remotely connected with the unbridled fury I experienced now. I continued to pound the bag until both my arms ached, but I unleashed another full-scale attack which lasted until I fell to the floor, writhing in pain at the severe cramps in my arms. I couldn't move them at all, but in my mind, it dawned on me that I was the meanest man on the planet.

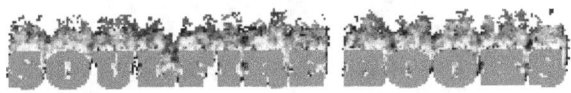

FIGHT NIGHT!

I quickly chose a spot to focus upon. It was a tiny niche, in the distance just under the glare of the lights. The elegant man had told me that when I emerged from the dressing room with my entourage en route to the ring to ignore the crowd and the noise. I couldn't afford to be distracted, but the noise was deafening. On either side of me were walls of people. I was so attuned that I could smell the cigarette smoke and countless brands of perfume and cologne. The flash of the cameras lit the joint up like white-hot firecrackers, searing my eyes.

I pushed myself through the ropes and quickly crossed over to the other side, throwing jabs and hooks at the air, delighting the immense crowd. I was the undercard of a championship middleweight fight.

"You're on your own in there," the elegant man whispered. "That's the way you wanted it, and that's the fucking way it will be, This ain't gonna be no cakewalk. That motherfucker is hungry."

"Anything else?" I snapped.

"Yeah, by the way it is." The elegant man looked serious. "No matter how bad he is beating you, I ain't throwing the towel in."

He meant it.

I crouched down on my stool, listening to all the last minute instructions from my handlers. My nerves felt electric, but outwardly, I displayed no emotions. I glanced up and out. Everything seemed so vast and gaping, so I quickly brought my focus back to the ring where everything was smaller and more contained. It seemed safer because it was a place where you couldn't get lost. Your opponent would make sure of that.

Abruptly, I was summoned to the center of the ring. The other fighter was there when I got there, looking like he was ready. The referee provided us with the house rules, bade us to touch gloves and then to come out fighting at the bell.

Seconds later: DING!

We met precisely in the middle of the ring, peeking murderously over our gloves. He shot off a right jab that missed, then scrambled a bit to the side. It was an awkward move, and I plowed into him with a couple of body shots. He landed a short left hook to my chin. For the next fifteen seconds, we fought viciously at the same spot, only our arms and legs moving, our feet seemed cemented to the canvas. We battled as though we were heavily in debt to all these yelling spectators. We knew exactly what they wanted; Blood.

He tried to kill me.

I tried to kill him.

End of round one.

For the second round, I disappointed my opponent by not meeting him in the center of the ring. Instead, I settled into my fight plan, floating in and out of his reach, using the ring to my advantage. In front of his corner, he trapped me, and viciously tagged me with a left/right combo which he followed with a thundering hook to my body. It crashed into my ribs, and the sudden impact seemed to explode one of my internal organs, making me lower my guard involuntarily. The price for this was a stiff overhand right that knocked me back into the ropes. He swarmed all over me, throwing punches without letting up, connecting on almost every blow.

The crowd roared when he knocked me down.

I had sense enough, though badly shaken, to rest on one knee until the count of eight before getting up to face the referee who asked if I was alright. He then wiped my gloves on his shirt, and jump-started the fight. Over his shoulder, my foe appeared larger and stronger than ever, and just as soon as the referee had moved away, depriving me of his protection, I found myself feebly attempting to ward off the attack. I was feeling lightheaded, the gloves were heavy as I faced a moment of defenseless terror.

I was saved by the bell.

At least this time, the people in my corner had their work cut off for them. They were busy trying to revive me, to stimulate my senses, but to my estimation, they had not done enough for me by the time the bell sounded for the next round. I had some trouble staying on my toes, so I decided to fight flat-footed, to clinch and to tie him up as much as I could in an effort to slow the pace of the round down to a crawl. At the time, I was not trying to win points, but room to breathe.

He did it again. Was it a response to something I did, or did he just do it out of habit? Anyway, before I could decide, he hammered me with a hook that twisted my head around so violently that I coughed up my mouthpiece. The ref kicked it aside.

I fought back as he waded in, and for a good portion of the next ten seconds, we exchanged such damaging blows that they brought the thrill-seeking crowd to its feet. Their screams for blood rent the high heavens.

When I moved my right arm down to block a feint to my mid-section, I had finally solved the riddle of his awkward scrambling to the side. He was trying to slip into position to fire away with a hook to my head while my guard was lowered. He was always a fraction of a second too slow.

There was something about this realization that gave me renewed enthusiasm, providing me with the authority to exercise my newfound power over him. He smashed a fist into my nose which made me realize that I had better find a way to exploit this weakness before it was too late. He hit me in face with another jab.

I stepped in quickly, clinching, pulling him to me, and leaning my entire weight on him, hoping to tire him out. The referee moved in to separate us.

"Fight!" he commanded.

I weaved a punch or two, threw a punch or two of my own, and then wrapped my opponent up in another bear hug, leaning all my body weight on him. Once more, I held on, ignoring the referee's barking orders to break. I made him work for his pay. I made him separate us.

Shuffling backwards, I held my right hand high, just under my chin. As he came at me, I slowed, letting him chase me. In the middle of his jab, I lowered my right hand. This halted the completion of his jab, and he almost lost his balance as he tried to scoot into position to throw the hook. I slowly raised the hand back into position.

I smelled it coming, the feint to my body. He was ready, but so was I. This time, I kept the right hand raised high, dropping it at the very last second to entice him. He went for it! He scrambled to his right even before he had pulled his right hand back up to sufficiently protect himself. This left the entire side of his face totally exposed, an open target.

Everything moved in slo-mo now, and in what seemed like forever, I managed to get my hands up, and split the air with a menacing hook that whistled. I saw his arms rising frantically to meet and to intercept the punch, to protect his vulnerable jaw and chin. Both of our eyes met as the collision came.

Suddenly, I was rocketed back into real time by the voice of the referee who was loudly ordering me to a neutral corner. I recognized his excessively loud counting.

"One.......Two........Three."

My opponent moved dazedly.

"Four.........Five."

He was on one knee.

"Six.........Seven.......Eight.

He was pushing himself upwards.

"Nine.........."

He toppled back to the canvas.

"It's over!" The ref yelled. "He's out!"

I had passed the first test of my journey, and I felt that no celebration was in order. It was simply one win. I wanted to leave it at that.

On my way out of the ring, I had barely given the elegant man a passing glance. Of all my handlers, it was obvious that he had given up on me in the second round. It was no big deal. Thrusting my hands out at him defiantly, I demanded that he cut the gloves off.

"Throw them away," I snarled when they were off.

"Keep them," my trainer pleaded. "A memento to your first fight, a tribute------."

"Throw them away," I gruffly repeated. "I'm on a mission. Ain't got time for no mementos, no memories, shit like that. I'm a champion, not a collector."

The elegant man chuckled. "Mighty big talk."

"And it's coming from a winner," I snapped quickly. "A winner who gonna keep right on winning."

"You got lucky in there. You were dead in the water. That nigger had you outgunned by a mile."

"And got knocked out." It was the trainer speaking. "For once, I wish you two would stop bickering. It ain't good for the morale of the other fighters. Ain't we all on the same team?" The trainer stalked off.

Being alone with the elegant man made me uncomfortable. He was still attractive, but that wasn't it. I was over the earlier sexual attraction I had felt for him. That was a fling from my youth. Plus, I now actually considered him old, and that was definitely a turn-off. But what did intrigue me about the elegant man was that he had power. That may have been an understatement because I was convinced that, standing on his own, the elegant man had no clout, but he was connected well enough that he could persuade others to do what he wanted or needed done. I bristled at how easily he had gotten me shipped off to the Army. He would pay for that one day. I would decide when, of course.

"Temporary truce," the elegant man said brightly, extending his hand.

I played along. I shook his hand.

"There is someone who wants to meet you."

I instantly recoiled, snatching my hand away angrily. "No."

"No?" he replied. "You don't even know who it is."

"It doesn't matter who it is. Tell him to get lost."

"Hey now," the elegant man smiled, "I thought we had a truce going on here."

"What I just agreed to doesn't include entertaining your friends and associates."

139

Now, the elegant man spoke more severely. "There are some people that you don't say no to."

I laughed. "That's how I once felt about Santa Claus. Thank God, I grew out of that foolishness." I looked at him sincerely. "With a little help, it may be possible for you to rid yourself of your awe for people. No is a word that everybody gotta deal with sometimes in their lives."

The elegant man gripped my arm tightly, his eyes blazing with rage. "Do not mistake your importance to us," he said forcibly, pushing my arm away. "I'm going to cover for you this time, but remember not to make the same mistake twice."

"Sounds like a threat, if you ask me."

"It is. Make no mistake about that."

I smirked, "You sure have grown in the last few years. Gone from a child molester to a big, bad terminator."

The motherfucker slapped me.

"I'm going to overlook that this time, but remember not to make the same mistake again. The next time, you'll pay dearly."

"You really don't get it, do you?' He took a deep breath to calm himself down. "You have yet to grasp the dimensions of what this is all about." He looked grief-stricken. "Whatever you may think it is, well, it's bigger, better, and more wonderful."

He left me standing there.

I didn't dare imagine what the totality of The Talented Xth encompassed. Routinely, I just concentrated on what they wanted me to do. Now, that I was actually involved with them, I went numb. Just what was I involved with totally? So much was unknown. I tried to point out to myself just what I did know, and I felt silly because I knew virtually nothing.

Well, practically, nothing.

2

"No one runs The Talented Xth," the mean ol' Army man wisecracked. "The Talented Xth runs itself and that's what so nice about it. Everyone knows their job, and they do it. Nothing could be any simpler. The Talented Xth simplifies everything. What we do is to break everything down to its most basic components, and then we let the person who sees the big picture the clearest handle the situation. This is much better than trying to train someone to do the job and it beats the hell out of guesswork."

"But what can you do?'

"Well, say for example, we decided we wanted to inconvenience the general population, we could shut off all the electricity in virtually every metro area of the country." He winked. "We do that from time to time."

"And you do that just for kicks?"

"Nothing in war is for fun as you very well know, but yes, we derive a sort of perverted thrill simply knowing that we have such a skilled corps of engineers in place to do that sort of thing. It comes in handy when an especially annoying homophobe is appearing on TV to give an interview or speech or what have you, we deny him air time by simply disrupting his broadcast or by shutting the power off completely. Impressed?"

"Not hardly," I scoffed. "So, you got a few tricks, but it will never be enough to induce change. To win a war, sir, you have to be able to do more than slightly inconvenience your enemy." I winced. "See, I wasn't asleep in military class all the time."

"Where is your vision, youngster. Do you know that while gays make up only about ten percent of the population in this country, we comprise the most talented segment of the professional sector----."

"At least, now I know how you guys came about the name," I slyly remarked.

He ignored me. "That means that the pulse of this country is in our hands. We run the banks, the hospitals, the military, and little does the general population know about it."

"Now, that's something to consider." I winked. "Got anything else?"

"What else!?" His voice was strained. "What else!? Heavens only knows what else. One well-placed word from the right member of our team and all the research on the next wonder drug will come to a screeching halt. No questions asked. Or we could cause a screw-up of all the patients waiting on liver transplants and kill off a third of them on the waiting list due to the delay. We can wreak havoc on this country's infrastructure, its medical supplies."

Now, I was impressed.

"One of our novelty area is the maternity wards." His eyes glistened with pride. "We can destroy any baby born in the country, so whenever one of the prejudiced, bigoted gay-basher has a baby, they place that child's life at our mercy even if they don't know it. We could snuff their son or daughter out and make it appear congenital. That," he said proudly, "is the kind of power we have."

"Then why haven't you used it?"

"You don't simply use your power just because you have it. Power is not an advertisement for 'here-I-come-ready-or-not'. Power, even with all that it is, must await its proper moment, that one moment when it will be most potent; most destructive."

"But what of in the meanwhile?"

"Life goes on. We continue to quietly position our troops, moving everything in place so that when the moments arrives, the triumph of The Talented Xth will be complete and unmistakable."

"But who decides the moment," I persisted.

"Destiny!" he declared.

142

I didn't have to say anything, but I knew the Army man agreed with my silence. After all, he was military so he knew that every mission had to have a timetable, an exact point in time for its precise execution. In his heart, the Army man knew that The Talented Xth couldn't continue to go on this way without the weakness being detected. There was no conceivable way for it to continue going unnoticed or unprotested forever. One other thing he also knew was that with that kind of concentrated power, many in The Talented Xth were eager to use it, to test it; to fiddle around and to tinker with it.

Someone had to be willing to assume responsibility for establishing an operable timetable, and to push things through to its pre-determined conclusion. I knew that person would have to be me.

"Haven't enough gays in this country been discriminated against? Isn't homophobia on the rise?" I looked him in the eyes. "What in the hell are you waiting for?"

He sighed wistfully. "At any given moment, The Talented Xth has the combined national capacity to bring the country to its knees. We can disrupt any vital industry in this country, can cause gridlock on all the major highways, can contaminate the world's food supply. And yet we do nothing."

I had to take over The Talented Xth!

3

Over the next year, I fought twice, handily winning both by knockouts. I was beginning to gain recognition as a professional, and beyond the unheeded objections of the elegant man was winning on my own merits and I was battling top-notch fighters. Even at the distance I now stood from a championship fight, if I continued to be impressive in the ring, they would be forced to give me a shot.

I was on a mission. I no longer indulged myself in the mind-blowing oohs and aaahs of the flesh because they were detours. With little or no regrets, I slammed the door to the passageway of passion for nothing must stop me from the command of The Talented Xth.

But The Talented Xth was so mysterious?

I knew it was a dangerous thing to do, but I was hungry to get to the bottom of this enigma so I could get to the top of it. I approached the elegant man.

"Let's not pretend," I suggested as we ate lunch in a small French café who served delicious croissants, "I'm going to ask certain questions, and I hope to get at least a straightforward answer in return."

"My, my, my." The elegant man lisped, "just listen to you. At long last, you have learned to string together ideas and formulate them into complete sentences minus profanity. I'm impressed." He nodded. "The military really polished you up, made a man of sorts out of you."

"The Army didn't do shit for me------."

"You're such a sucker for a compliment," the elegant complained. "Give you a sincere one and you fall to pieces, beating yourself over the head to prove you haven't changed, that you're still as tough as nails. Being cultured and refined has never weakened a man, you little snot-nosed punk."

I raised my hand.

The elegant man was calm. "I have a weapon and I will use it. Of that, be sure." He took a sip of his water. "Anger is so unbecoming to you. Go to the little boys' room and compose yourself. You look a mess."

My head was spinning with dizziness. I could scarcely see straight, and it appeared as if the elegant man was fumbling around inside his jacket. I was so mixed up at the moment that it did seem wise to get away from the table. Hesitantly, I slowly stood up, and then rushed to the bathroom.

I was grateful that the bathroom was empty. Without delay, I instantly began to shadowbox, breathing in and out deeply as I threw punches, watching myself in the mirror, trying to drain the anger out of my face. Seconds later, I doused my face with stinging needles of cold water.

I went back out.

"Ah, so you didn't skip out of the back," the elegant man mused coolly. "I admire a man with balls.' He pointed an accusing finger at me. "You must learn to take your whippings like a man."

"And just who the fuck are you pretending to be offering all this great advice. You a sultan or something?"

The elegant man laughed. "It's just that you have underestimated me for all these years. Somehow, you got locked into a certain image of me and this is what you have held on to. You formed an opinion of me as some old gym rat who secretly lusted off the boxers. In your mind, you probably believed that I was an old sissy who lived to run to the gym and to smell the sweat of young niggers. Well, you were wrong."

"I'll leave it to you to make more of yourself if that's what you like. Personally, I see no proof of you being important."

His laughter was sparkling. "I'll let you be the judge of that later so come on, let's get down to brass tacks. Come straight to the point," he intoned coldly. "Just what the fuck do you want?"

"Answers!?" I yelled as loud as I could without attracting attention. "I want answers. I want answers about you know what and I want them today, or I'm out."

"You're such a childish individual," the elegant man said softly. "If you don't get your way, you're going to take your toys and go home. You probably did that as a kid. Well, this is somewhat different. No one gives a fuck about how much you pout or throw a temper tantrum. Well, you almost saw, a few minutes ago, what a temper tantrum will get you." He patted the outside of his jacket.

I casually stacked up my dirty dishes and then pushed them away. I wanted something to do with my hands. Somewhat bitterly, I wiped them clean with a damp napkin, and the elegant man watched.

"Just what answers are you in search of?" The voice was patient and calm, denoting emptiness. He knew what was being asked of him.

Seeing that he was having no problem with being gracious, I observed him meaningfully. "Does this have an end date or does The Talented Xth keep right on wrecking lives?"

"Wrecking lives?!" He looked at me insanely, turning the question over and over in his head. "Whose lives?"

"The lives of all of us who believe that we are going to make a difference. I find it irresponsible to keep all of us in suspended animation without a clear forecast of what is due when."

"Why don't you just concentrate on winning the championship. I bet that would speed the timetable up a whole helluva lot."

"So, I'm the key."

"What you are is a catalyst. Yes, a lot hinges on you, but----
----."

"Stop lying, dammit. It's me."

The elegant man softened. "Don't quote me on this, but from everything I'm led to believe, everything is gearing towards a big event."

"And you think that night is the night I win the title?"

146

"Your announcement, or if you will, renouncement is what's important. Can't you see it?" he prattled excitedly. "Geared to this cataclysmic moment, we will spring into action while the world is still reeling from the shock of your news. We'll crash the stock market the following morning, cut off the water, and drown the nation in total darkness by turning off the power." He stopped himself. "You didn't hear any of this from me. Anyway, if I were you, I'd step up my training regimen because your next opponent is one of the best in the division."

I wondered how much of this was I to believe.

With so much expected of me, I wasn't in the mood to be caught with my pants down so I decided to go to New York to speak with an Army buddy who had snagged a job on Wall Street once his tour of duty was complete. We had lunch in Manhattan.

"Now, let me get this right," my friend asked, "you came all the way to New York to see someone you haven't seen in ages, and you only had a single question about Wall Street." He glared at me glumly. "Something is up, and it's real and it is imminent or else you wouldn't be sitting here, trying to hide your nervousness." He grinned. "You know what gave you away?"

I said nothing.

"You never asked how it could be done. You asked if the market could be manipulated which leads me to believe that you know how it can be done. All you wanted was confirmation that the scheme would work. That's what gave you away. If this was strictly dinner conversation, right after I told you that it could indeed be done, your very next question should have been how. You never asked."

I squeezed out an agitated chuckle.

"As a friend, I must warn you that tampering with the stock market is a federal crime, but I'm sure your colleagues already know this." He grinned at me lopsidedly. "What have you gotten yourself into, old Army pal?" He waved his hand to stop an answer. "You're a big boy and can handle yourself." He extended his hand. "For both of our sakes, this conversation never happened."

I gripped the hand tightly. "Thanks, pal."

Leaving the eatery, I decided to stay in New York overnight. With nothing but time on my hands, I was certain that I could find something to do in the greatest city in the world. Instead, I checked into a hotel, jumped in bed with my clothes on, curled up in the fetal position, and took a nap.

Upon awakening, I flicked ON the TV and received the biggest surprise yet. My Army pal was dead! There he was, his face plastered across the evening news in full color. Dead! Apparently, the newswoman reported, he had been the victim of a senseless robbery. Of course, I didn't buy it. Okay, yes, my Army pal whom I'd just lunched with earlier, was dead, but the murder didn't have a thing to do with a stinking robbery.

I bolted from the hotel in a flash.

Once I was finally able to locate a cabbie brave enough to drive me to Harlem, the quest to find safe lodgings became my primary focus. For once, luck was on my side.

What the old, dilapidated Harlem hotel lacked in appeal, it made up for by allowing me a more secure frame of mind. Even The Talented Xth wouldn't fuck around on 125th Street, the black mecca; the capitol of all the ghettoes in America.

The phone rang!

I nearly jumped out of my skin. No one knew where I was. No one should be calling........

"Wh-who is this?"

"Stop acting stupid. Stop trying to run. It is such a waste of everyone's time---and patience. Just relax," the elegant man mumbled. "Since you're there, go to The Club and have a good time. For you, everything is on the house. Just make sure that I see you bright and early tomorrow. Before noon."

Everything about The Club reeked of debauchery, and everyone on the inside of the place was working extra hard to make sure it remained that way. No one had even the slightest intention of not being at their most sordid and perverse best, but it all was accomplished with satirical elegance.

I transformed myself into a voyeur. I observed from as comfortable a distance as the surroundings would permit, but I was vaguely unsettled by the way that no matter where I was, I always seemed to standing on the verge of being sucked involuntarily into the celebration. Here, the orgy came to you!

Even though I was no longer depressed over the death of my Army pal, I was slightly offended when my pants were unzipped and I felt strange lips upon my privates. Personally, I liked to be begged…………,but oh my!

I was truly annoyed, when hours later, a large hand gripped my arm, disengaging me from party of four.

"It's time for you to leave," the burly bouncer spoke gruffly, stuffing a small envelope into my hand. "You booked on a mid-morning flight. Don't miss it. Go get some sleep because someone will pick you up when the time comes." He steered me towards the door. "Good night and happy landing."

I was up early the next morning, laughing cheerfully at how easily my resolve had been destroyed. I thought I had weaned myself from lust, but now realized I was only stalling, awaiting the right temptation.

"Whew! I moaned loudly, thinking back to last night, and then after quelling the near riot of sexual memories that exploded inside my head. I calmed down. I still had to face the elegant man.

FUCK HIM!

For some reason, I was not afraid of the elegant man. Nor did it bother me to view him as a flunky, as someone I could handle by myself. I had cozied up to that notion a long time ago, and couldn't shake it despite the things that had been done through him. I imagined that most of his harmlessness stemmed from the fact that he had been in bed with me, and like Mother I felt that any man I had made love to was helplessly at my mercy. And of all the men that Mother and I had been with, this old one should be no exception.

149

The motherfucker hit me!

As soon as the plane had landed, the elegant man and two other men were there awaiting my arrival. As soon as I disembarked, I headed onto the concourse where the trio emerged out of the scattering crowd and clambered up beside me. Then the elegant man, without warning or speaking, punched me viciously in the kidney. The unexpected blow doubled me over.

"Bitch, you so much as bat a motherfucking eyelash and I'll plug you so full of holes, you won't be able to hold water." He gripped my chin in his hands roughly and squeezed. The pressure was immense, feeling as though he was going to cave a tooth in on both sides of my mouth.

"Oww!" I groaned without embarrassment.

"Shut the fuck up," the elegant man ordered, "or I'll kill you on the spot. He pushed my face away angrily, then before I knew it had slapped me with the back of his hand. "That's right, punk, get mad." He pushed me in the chest. "C'mon, get mad. You mad yet, you red-assed nigger?" He reached into his jacket. "Get mad, motherfucker, and die."

I stood mute.

He nodded at his goons. "Let's go. Get him out of my face before I finish his ass off."

They escorted me through the terminal, steering me this way and that by a mere tap on my elbow or a nod of the head. I looked like a tiny doll between them. The elegant man walked behind us, unsmiling.

Already, I wished I could undo the trip to New York. That way, my Army pal would still be alive, and I would know where I was going. Out of the terminal, I was forced into a dark sedan, and my interest in where I was going became more acute. I made a polite inquiry.

The response. "You'll know when you get there."

"Where is the elegant man?"

"He'll be there when you get there. Now, shut the fuck up."

Unused to being taken somewhere against my will, everything started to feel more and more scary. I had been caught with my 'draws" down, and my mind was beginning to

150

taunt me with the possibility of death, or if not that, brutal violence. After all, my Army pal was died. Why spare me? When my mind couldn't conjure up an argument to that very vital question, my heartbeat throbbed at a pace that was unnatural.

"Where you taking me?" I was more emphatic this time.

"Weren't you told to be quiet?"

"I don't care. If you're going to kill me, just as well do it now because I'm not being quiet. I want to know WHERE I'M GOING?!

"I told you that you would know when you got there." He was more emphatic this time as he slipped on a pair of black gloves. "Any more questions?"

My throat was dry. I swallowed. "I bet you can't beat me by yourself."

He grunted.

"None of you can, one on one. Stop the car," I pleaded, "and I'll fight one of you. Naw, I'll fight both of y'all one at a time. If I win, y'all let me go."

"What if one of us wins?"

I took a deep breath. "Then you can kill me."

The driver swung the car off the road and down a dusty lane. "We here. Get the fuck out."

I was forced into a greenhouse that was filled with flowers and plants. I was led past tiers of exotic specimens and between rows of expensive hybrids, and then shoved into a darkened office at the back.

A figure in a cloak and hood sat immobile at a desk hunched over a rose, fingering it lovingly. The elegant man scowled at me while the figure in the hood and cloak did not look up or away from the rose. He lightly stroked a petal brushing the tip of his finger gently across the flower's expanse.

"Beautiful," he confessed before looking upon me for the first time. "You need to grow roses." He was speaking to me. "That way you would understand the delicacy of cultivating something that is perfect. A lot goes into the end results, just like this mission of ours which is a work under cultivation." He coughed to alert me to pay close attention to what was next said. "If one person decides to strike out on his own, or to ask unnecessary questions, then, well, problems arise." The voice was clear. "I have been made aware of your disappointment with the snail's pace at which things seem to be moving, but trust me, nothing is amiss. The Talented Xth is not a headless horseman."

"I just thought----."

"You are in no position to do any thinking within the organization." The hooded figure laughed. "I'm sorry that all the thinking jobs were taken." He then turned serious. "You were allowed in as a performer, but don't slight your role. A lot hinges on it." He spoke to the elegant man. "He knows how much is riding on him, doesn't he?"

"He knows," the elegant man rasped.

He faced me, the hood falling down further on his shadowed face. "And still you stick your nose in places where it doesn't belong. Your snooping mocks us, and we do not tolerate insolence. You committed a grave offense, and by your carelessness, you caused an accident in New York." His tone softened. "You didn't want anyone meddling in your boxing career, now did you?"

"No sir."

"Why?"

"Because I know I'm capable of getting the job done without any interference."

"My sentiments exactly when it comes to the overall affairs of The Talented Xth. We don't need any meddling because we are sufficiently capable. Understood?"

"Yes."

"Well, for your next fight, the elegant man is going to handle things."

"No!?" I yelled. "Why?"

The hooded figure and the elegant man stood to leave. "Because you may not be completely recovered by then."

The goons pounced on me like white on rice.

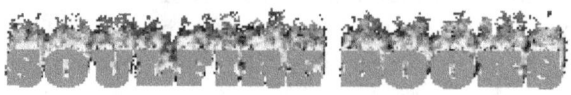

It was two o'clock when I woke up, and the little beeping machine I was hooked up to was glowing green, and making intricate patterns across the flat black monitor.

I didn't like hospitals.

A nurse with bedroom eyes hovered over my bed. "Comfy?"

I nodded in response.

"Good," she said as she left the room.

I gingerly rolled back the sheets from my body and visually examined myself. Nothing appeared to be broken or severely damaged. I became instantly happy. And then I got a visitor.

"Red-assed nigger, you should be dead." It was the elegant man.

"Is that how you usually greet people? With threats?"

He stood over the bed. "If it was left up to me, it wouldn't be a threat or anything you perceive as a threat. It would be a done deed." He leaned into my face, his voice sinister. "I wanted to take your life." He stood erect. "I wanted to make sure that you knew this."

The elegant man was serious, and given the chance he would have murdered me, and nothing could disguise the fact that he wanted to do so now. Recognizing this, I began to feel uneasy and noticed that I had unconsciously began to squirm in the bed, flinching slightly every time his hand moved.

"What-what have I ever done to you to make you hate me so much? I thought we had something," I lied.

"Along with your Mother's good looks, I see you also inherited her conceit. Just like her, you probably figure that every man who gets into your pants is your sucker for life. I thank myself for having had you pegged a long time ago. That's right, red-assed bitch, I saw you coming. When you first told me you were gay that night, and after we were together, I knew then I had to be careful. I recognized the danger of standing too fucking close to your pretty fire. I knew that all your life, you had grown up watching how your Mama made men beg and grovel at her feet, and I knew that you had subconsciously picked up the lessons, learned a trick or two here and there, and that you would not hesitate to use them. Who wouldn't?"

I was blinded by the pain in his eyes, but it was then that I knew. Yet I chose to say nothing.

The elegant man turned his back to me. "Your Mother was the most beautiful woman I had ever seen in my life and believe me, I've seen dames all over the fucking world." He spun around quickly, facing me. "But none of them could hold a candle to your Mama. She was the only woman on God's green earth that ever made me curse being gay. That's right, red nigger, I wanted your Mother. Just like every other man in town who wasn't blind, crippled, or crazy, I wanted to fuck your Mama. I dreamed of sticking my face between her legs for as long as she would let me, and when she sent me home, I would proudly beg, borrow, steal; anything to get her to let me do it again. But here I am, a fucking faggy who had to run away from the only woman that I have had wet dreams over, the only woman I had sexual desires for. And then guess what the fuck happens. You! You fall into my lap like some priceless jewel, and this unexpected gift of you exceeded the epitome of anything I could have ever wished for in my lifetime. Through you, I had a piece of your Mama." He got angry for no reason. "Red-assed nigger, when I was fucking you, it wasn't really you I was fucking. It was-------."

"My Mother."

"Who else? Did you think that you, a little, snot-nosed punk, actually deserved that special kind of tender love and gentle passion. Hell no," he jeered. "Every time I fucked you, you were just a reasonable facsimile of the person I really wanted. I fucked you like I wished I could have fucked your Mama. Oh, my goodness," he groaned.

"But Mother is dead, I purred softly.

"I know that, dammit," he cursed bitterly.

"Here I am, though." I threw open my arms.

"Oh yes," he cried. "Oh my goodness. Yes"

I sat down in front of the elegant man, and stared out onto the dance floor. Well-wishers were still waving from across the room. Dressed-up woman blew kisses. The band played loudly. One man whom I noticed earlier crossed in front of the bandstand and came strolling over. He slapped me on the back heartily.

"Great fight. You were superb. I'm in your corner, Champ."

"Well, I'm not champ, yet," I remarked humbly.

"You will be as soon as they stop ducking you and give you a shot at the title."

"Thanks," I said.

Another man approached the table. He handed the elegant man a camera and then quickly motioned to a woman who stood off to the side, a short distance away. "C'mon honey," he bellowed giddily, "let's take a picture with the next heavyweight champion of the world."

Later, the owner of the club grandly led a stunningly attractive woman to our table, and both the elegant man and I stumbled clumsily to our feet to be introduced.

"I enjoyed your fight," she marveled.

"Since when do beautiful Hollywood movie stars find the time to do something ordinary." I said smiling.

"I find nothing about you ordinary," she replied smartly. She pressed a card into my hand. "If you're ever in Los Angeles." She waved goodbye.

"Bitch." The elegant man watched her walk away. "Let's go. That hussy just spoiled my night."

"You're jealous."

"I saw the way you looked at her. What do you expect?"

"For you to know better?"

The elegant man fished in his pocket. "Here." He pushed a miniature-sized, oblong box across the table at me.

"What is it?"

"Look and see."

It was a ring.

"I know it's a little early, but when this is all over, will you marry me?"

"Marry you?" I was shocked, but that was just the beginning.   There   was   more.

"But not as a man------."

I wished that I could have seen the expression on my face.

"I-I want you to undergo a complete sex change," he continued. "I will pay for everything. This way we can go somewhere quiet and live together normally." He grinned sheepishly. "I promise to be good to you."

I almost laughed in his face. This motherfucker still had a fetish for Mother, and I wasn't about to try to live up to that. He'd have to go somewhere else for that kind of wish fulfillment. I didn't tell him that, though.

In all honesty, because it would be misleading, I can't truthfully say that the elegant man was pussy-whupped, but he was whipped just the same. Call it what you want; dazed, dazzled, cum-drunk, he was all that plus some, and I had him wrapped around my lil finger. I made him do what I wanted him to do, and I loved making him beg.

The two biggest thrills in my life were provided by men. I enjoyed knocking them out in the ring, and I loved making them beg in bed. Both of these guilty pleasures made me cum in my pants.

So, I was like my Mother. With a role model like that, how could I not get what I wanted. I no longer felt like dying when I got weak in the knees at the sight of a handsome young man, and thought that I couldn't have him. Once I got rid of that asinine notion, I disrupted a good number of happy households. Mother would have been so proud.

I treaded my way between men with such finesse that none of them paid any attention to how trapped they were in my web until I stopped meeting them for dinner, or no longer returned their calls. Then, once it became clear that I was finished with them, as if on cue, the begging would start. It was so delicious. Nothing much compares to the full, throaty whimpering of a jilted lover with a hard dick. Too me, that was PLEASURE!

I admit that sometimes there was a certain comedy to a big, full-grown man, kneeling butt-naked on the floor, licking my feet and sucking my toes that made me bubbly with laughter inside, but after a moment or two, the erotic suggestiveness of his total submission too me wreaked with raw passion.

Even the elegant man was at ease with my fooling around. He understand that he could do nothing about it, so his acceptance was a matter of course.

"Please don't ever turn me away," he had pleaded one night. "Please. I can take anything except that." He placed his mouth in the small of my back, running his tongue languidly over the curve of my butt. "I don't know what I'd do if you ever left me." He rolled me over onto my back. "We're still going to get married one day, you just wait and see." He rested his hand on my stomach and stared dreamily at the ceiling. "When I get finished re-making you, you are going to be a fantasy come true. You've already got the perfect ass," he chuckled, "and I want you to have big breasts also." He looked at me cautiously. "That's alright with you, isn't it?"

"Look." I said sweetly, "you know what I want?"

"What, sweetheart, what?"

I gently stroked his head, and smiled. "I want you to stop feeling like I'm a puppet for The Talented Xth. If I'm important to them like you say, then introduce me to them. I want to be a part of the inner circle, honey. I want you to open doors for me. You're my sweet daddy, right?" I rolled him over on top of me. "You'll do that for your baby, won't you, baby?"

I experienced his body going limp, but after I kissed him, it surged with power and strength.

"I promise," he promised, "I'll do it."

I smiled. Men loved telling me yes.

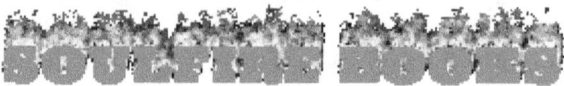

Of all the words in the universe, YES carries the most generous provisions. I could think of no other word that has a greater renown than YES when it came to opening doors previously closed to you, or closing doors on people who had refused to open doors for you.

It is almost beyond my comprehension how much difference this one, solitary word can make because whenever you look out into the vast audience of the A-B-C-s, Y-E-S are the crowned princes of the English language.

On stage, I looked out into the multitude of faces, and quickly reviewed my rehearsed speech. I made the crowd wait for a few more seconds while I purposely sought out the face of the elegant man and smiled happily at him.

"Boxing is so much easier than this," I coyly lied, "so I ask all of you to ignore my stage fright. Anyway, I, first must acknowledge that I am a proud member of The Talented Xth. I am also proud to be gay and I salute the day when the world will give us the respect that is due to us. One great day in the morning, it will be possible to flaunt our beautiful selves in public------."

The crowd roared cheerfully.

I graciously waited on the noise to die down then continued speaking. "When I was a child, my Mother taught me that the most tragic thing that could possibly happen to a person is for that person to have lived and that no one ever knew they had been here. In essence, we must leave our mark; our lives must count for something and with that great mantra in mind, I am proud to announce that in six months, I WILL BE THE HEAVYWEIGHT CHAMPION OF THE WORLD!"

Everyone exploded in wild applause. They whooped it up. I half-heartedly tried to talk over the deafening din. "An agreement was made between both camps this morning." No one actually heard me as their major preoccupation at the moment was merely to stomp their feet and to clap their hands more loudly.

I beamed, and for the first time discovered a third thrill that I got from men that made me cum in my pants. Now, in addition to knocking men out and making men beg, I got off on their adoration.

Applause made my nature rise.

The celebration was still in high gear when I was secretly whisked away, and driven across town a short distance to a very chic hotel. The elegant man and I were escorted to a dark, comfortable conference room filled with stern-faced men.

Seats were pointed out, and the elegant man and I occupied them, sitting directly across from each other on opposite sides of a rich, mahogany table.

Everyone present nodded, or otherwise acknowledged the elegant man, who, in turn, appeared to be, at least, vaguely familiar with all those seated around the table.

For a few seconds after we were seated, a polite patter of conversation continued until it was abruptly halted by the distinguished, white-haired gentleman seated at the head of the table. He glared at me briefly, then grinned solemnly. "So, we finally meet." We were seated too far away to shake hands, so he nodded his head in my direction. I retuned the gesture.

"From your announcement earlier, I take it to mean that a verbal agreement has been reached." The white-haired gentleman waited expectantly. Anxious.

"Not simply a verbal agreement, sir," I responded boldly, "but a signed contract." I paused dramatically. "The fight is on."

A sharp, rippling current of electricity surged through the room.

"Do you know what this means?" the white-haired gentleman asked.

"Yes sir," I cracked, "it means that I will get a chance to beat the crap out of the current champion before millions and millions of viewers."

Hushed laughter erupted at this.

"I greatly admire your spunk."

"I am a winner," I boasted.

"And then so are we," the white-haired gentleman said, smiling kindly. "Don't get me wrong, because I'm not disputing you. No sir, not in the least. It means just what you said it means but," he cautioned firmly, "so much more." Then with sudden obvious thirst, he greedily gulped down the rest of the water, and solemnly replaced the empty glass on the bamboo placemat. He cleared his throat. "As you may or may not know, over the last few years, The Talented Xth has been frantic in its search for a jump-off point for our plans. We have, for some time, been in need of an event from which we could coordinate all of our activities. Of late, there have been some very combative debates over how to use this preemptive strike once we have identified and agreed upon it, so you see we here have been quite busy." He smiled paternally. "You have to know how extremely important this choice is, or will be since it will represent, to our standpoint, an action that once enacted will have no way of being throttled or stopped." He gasped for air, searching for his next words. "Once we expose our plans and unleash our programme upon the world, there will be no turning back. Once this mission is in effect, we must conquer----or be crushed. Do you understand?"

I did.

"That is exactly why it has been such a hot topic of debate. If any of our conclusions are wrong, or if we do not choose where to draw first blood carefully, then all of our interests, both privately and professional, not to mention our lives, will be in great peril." He spoke now in a slow, melodic drone. "But now," his voice rose sharply, "we are ready to unveil our plans for America." He stared directly at me. "Thanks to you," he announced grandly, "we will activate our plans on the night of your renouncement!"

I leaned back in my chair violently. It was as if a great burden had just been placed on my shoulders. I instantly felt faint.

"Are you okay?" the man seated next to me asked.

Another man dabbed perspiration from my brow.

"I'm fine," I protested, "I'll be okay."

"Now, you see precisely what it is I've been strapped with," the white-haired gentleman offered. "Sometimes it can be overwhelming. I personally assure that I understand, and while I sympathize with you, the decision has been made, ratified, and for all practical purposes, etched in stone."

"I-I-I."

"Once you refuse to be crowned and renounce the heavyweight title, you will read a prepared statement proclaiming you gayness and making a public declaration that discrimination against gays be deemed illegal, ceasing at once. And just as soon as you finish your dramatic statement, the entire country will be drenched in total darkness." The white-haired gentleman beamed. "I think they'll get the point, but if not, they will. The next day, the stock market will crash, throwing the country into a depression that will make the one in '29 seem like a Sunday school picnic." He saw the look of worry on my face. "Don't be alarmed, it won't last long. We only intend to induce widespread panic."

"But----."

"We will also disrupt the water supply, and force the country to do without the precious commodity for three days." The white-haired gentleman began to rant. "The fools in this country take water, as valuable as it is, for granted, just like they have taken the gays of this country for granted, but soon they shall see. They will be compelled, by circumstance, to reckon with us as equals" His voice rose even more, filled with bombast and fire. He pounded the table angrily with his face, causing the elegant man and others to jump nervously. "They will have this choice and this choice alone. They will deal with us as equals or as masters."

The   meeting   ended.

5

Time swept past.

In another 90 days, I would be fighting for the heavyweight championship of the world. Without doubt, I would win, and that would usher in the end of the world as we now knew it. I soul-searched myself because I didn't want what I was doing to be out of whack with what I was feeling. But what did I feel exactly? Numbness, mainly. By winning, I would be signing over the world to a new world order, but could I trust it?

Sometimes, I would get so paralyzed with fear just thinking of what would be, but what could I do now? I pondered on this issue until I ultimately reached the conclusion that there was nothing I could do------except win. And I would.

Even though, it was seldom said or whispered aloud except by a choice few, I knew The Talented Xth would not enter fight night without a Plan B. Too much was riding on this one night to entrust it entirely to my boxing prowess. They were too fearful that something could or would go wrong. One lucky punch could bring all their plans to a screeching halt, and they were too ill at ease to allow that.

"I must level with you," the elegant man told me, "but if, at any time during the fight. he hurts you, or somehow gets the upper hand, we will have no choice but dope his water bottle. It has already been arranged."

"So much for trust," I sneered.

"You must realize that you're not going out there to arm wrestle Mickey Mouse. This fight is for all the marbles." The elegant man sighed. "Circumstances compel us to take our precautions."

"Give me a chance to win the fight on my own," I pleaded. "I'm a fighter, he's a fighter and we're both going to get hit with some big shots, so please don't jump the gun on me, dammit. Give me a chance to do this on my own." When I saw a look of scorn cross the face of the elegant man, I angrily blurted. "Fuck you, you bastard. I see that I'll have to end this fight in the first fucking round."

"Stop dreaming," the elegant man laughed. "As you already know, the only thing you have to do is show up for the fight, and the rest is a foregone conclusion." He smirked. "It's simple. All we need is your presence in the ring, even if half-dead."

"Thanks, you bastard."

"Why do you make me tell you things that are only going to hurt you?" the elegant man huffed. "You know I don't like doing it, but you insist of forcing me to cause you pain."

"No pain, no gain," I cracked. "I'm in the best fucking physical conditioning of my life."

"It's not me, sweetheart, trust me. I wouldn't dream of doing anything to jeopardize you, but the wheels are in motion. At last, you have the timetable that you've demanded for so long. It's here, my love. It's all within reach."

I made a smacking sound with my lips. It was absolutely bitchy.

"Sweetheart," the elegant man rasped, "this is it, and you of all people should be pleased. Your place in the history of The Talented Xth is assured."

"The first hero of an enduring saga," I barked sarcastically. "Am I to be the George Washington of The Talented Xth?"

The elegant man grinned. "Hey, that's not a bad comparison because as you know, your name has been tossed about for a very high position in the organization------perhaps the top position. Who knows? No one will be able to dispute your credibility or visibility."

163

"Enough with the speechmaking. I don't need convincing because I know I'm fully capable and qualified to run this outfit and one day I will. I just need to keep my eyes on you and your old buddy network so y'all don't ruin shit before I get a shot at taking over." I glared coldly at the elegant man. "I'm looking for you to keep your friends in check."

About noon, I spotted the elegant man out of the corner of my eye, nervously wringing his hands, and whispering to one of the people in the gym. He stared in my direction a few times as he spoke, but otherwise didn't acknowledge me.

Once more he started towards where I sat at the ring's edge, but stopped suddenly and artfully pretended that something else was more urgent. For a full twenty seconds, he merely stood there examining his shoes until at last he decided they needed re-tying. He elegantly stooped over, untied one shoe and slowly re-did it. The other shoe required more of an operation because he had to kneel down on one knee to get it just right.

Ignoring everything around him, the elegant man gripped both ends of the shoestring and tugged tightly, pulling the laces tight. Then like a small child, he held each end up, comparing the length, measuring them against each other. The length was not quite precise, so he carefully made the necessary adjustment, loosening a bit on one end and feeding this slack to the other.

Once more, he took his measurement. This time. Perfect. And with nothing left to do, he quickly tied the shoe and stood.

I looked away, turning my head in another direction, but not so far that he was out of my vision. No doubt, I was intrigued. After wiping the knee of his pants off, he again headed in my general direction. I almost laughed aloud. He was zig-zagging, but after much too long, he made it beside my stool.

"Man," I bragged, "you should have seen the shit I put on my sparring partners today. I banged them up so bad, might have to put 'em out to pasture. I was beautiful in there today, baby……Awesome."

He gave me a weak, distracted pat on the back. "Good. Glad to hear that."

Inside, I was pumped up with curiosity as to why the elegant man was acting so strangely, but I refused to let on. I continued to prattle. "If you ask me, we better keep all sports reporters out from now on because if they leak this shit out about how good I'm looking in the ring, that chump champ might get scared and try to put the fight off. Motherfucker can sense when a real ass-whupping coming and they get scared as shit. Ain't that right?"

The elegant man said nothing.

"Remember, long time ago when you told me about that fighter down South who paid off some reporters to boost him up in the papers. Wasn't shit in the ring, but was a monster in print, terrifying. Motherfucking niggers in the other camp starting ready that phony shit and---."

The elegant man dismissed the episode with a wave of his hand. "Hurry up, shower and dress. I'm taking you somewhere."

From the tone of his voice, it dawned on me not to ask questions or to even be slow about performing the duties he had placed before me. He glanced at his watch as a further indication that time was of the essence.

"I'll wait in my car," he rasped hoarsely.

When I got into his car some minutes later, he again looked at his watch as though we were on the clock and was already tardy. He drove without speaking.

After three blocks of agitated silence, I was puzzled by his stoic patience, but I was ready to discover the nature of this trip. The direction in which we were travelling carried no information, so as we turned onto a street I was unfamiliar with, I simply laid back against the seat and closed my eyes. I was still paralyzed with curiosity, but no anxiety. By now, I was used to people wanting to meet me in private, away from the snooping noses of the public. Might as well get myself in the mood, I surmised, so I played with myself through my pants. Some of these old freaks just wanted to peek at my dick, or handle it for a few seconds before collapsing into spasms of quiet, sexual surrender.

The elegant man saw what I was doing, and firmly placed one of his hands over mine. He wasn't grinning. "It's not that."

165

It was then that I got frightened.

"What is it the fuck about, then?"

He stopped the car. "We're here. You'll find out for yourself."

A funeral home? Now, I was really puzzled.

Just before we got to the front door, I relaxed somewhat. I had worked it all out, everything had fallen into place of its own accord like clockwork. No wonder the long look on the elegant man's face.

"These things happen," I shrugged. "Your friend probably lived a good life." I opened the door. "Let's go in and pay our respects."

The elegant man stared at me unbelievingly. He snatched me back as if I was getting ready to step off a cliff. He gently closed the door. "Sweetheart, all my friends are well."

Who was in there, then?

Seeing me, the Other Woman ran the rest of the way up the steps. "I'm sorry," she stated, hugging me tightly. She reached for my hand. "Let's go in."

We entered the funeral parlor. It reeked of death, the scent of flowers, and the silence of people who grew frozen as I numbly followed the Other Woman to the front of the room where the casket was. On my way to view the body---someone's body---I became extremely anxious not to trip over my own feet as they fumbled across the carpet.

My vision was blurred. I was groggy because as I got close to the casket, I managed to pick out the faces of my brother, the pretty girl, and another young girl sitting between them. Their daughter, more than likely. Where was my bad-assed son, I half-wondered? In the bathroom? Outdoors? In another room? Anywhere......except in that casket!

I looked at the elegant man. He looked away. I looked down into the casket, and there was my boy.

The death of my son mystified me. I had, by no means, even been a good father to him and during his life I had harbored not even the slightest bit of affection for him, but seeing him dead like that touched a note of regret in me. The great drawback to this was that it was much too late for remorse, sympathy, or regret; and grief, in my case, would appear so trite and artificial.

"I-I really didn't think you would come, but I'm glad you did." It was the pretty girl. "I'm really glad you came."

I looked her over quickly, and she hadn't changed at all. She was still very pretty. I diverted my gaze. "Wh-what happened? Was he sick or something?"

The pretty girl shook her head slowly. "A car," she moaned pitifully. "He was killed by a car."

"A car? How? I know you didn't let him play in the streets." I stopped myself from talking. My voice was too strained. Plus, I had no right to question her, but still he had been my son.

"Of course, I didn't let him play in the streets and he was too smart to do it anyway. He was on this way from school and he got struck by a hit and run driver."

"Did---?"

"No, the driver was not caught."

"Damn," I cursed, my voice quavering. "Bet if it would have been a white kid." Again, I stopped talking. Where had I been all those years. Hell, I didn't even know how old he had been.

"He would have been seven this year, you know."

I could only sigh.

"I'll be out in the car," the elegant man said softly. He faced the pretty girl. "I'm sorry about your son."

"Is that the man who------."

"Yeah, that's him," I interrupted. "The man who took us to the abortion doctor that night."

"Let's walk outside," she prodded. "Did or has that man, your friend, ever said anything to you about that night?"

My eyebrows shot up. "Like what?"

"Oh, nothing much," the pretty girl admitted. "I was just wondering."

"Look," I said a little too loudly, "if something happened that night, I don't care what it was or how insignificant you might think it was, well, I want to know."

"That was almost seven years ago," she calmly replied, "why would it still be important?"

"Because I don't understand how you and a fucking stranger could ever have a secret that excluded me, especially on a night that was so important to us---me and you---and didn't, couldn't mean shit to him. That's why I want to know. Either you tell me now, or I will beat it out of him later."

"There you go with your tough man routine, thinking you can beat everyone up to get your way." The pretty girl stuck her chin out. "Why don't you beat me up to?"

"That's something I should have done when I got out of the Army."

"You abandoned me." She stuck her finger in my face. "You thought it was best for you to go off killing people in another country than to be at home with your own family." She glared at me spitefully. "How could you do that? I begged you to come home, but you wanted to keep on playing with your G.I. Joe guns some more, so I finally got fed up."

"So you jumped in bed with my brother?"

She tried to slap me, but I caught her hand mid-way.

"What do you care?"

"I care that our son is dead." The pretty girl looked like she wanted to spit in my face. "I cared," I mumbled.

"You didn't want him, remember. That's the reason why we went to the abortion doctor, remember? Our son is dead, right, but he got seven years of life, and I got that man, your friend, to thank for every minute of them."

"What did you say, bitch?"

"That's right, nigger," she spat. "If it hadn't been for your friend, our son would have never been born. He would have died that night. That's right, you dog, your friend set your no-good ass up so I could have my baby. That's right, Mister-Beat-Everybody-Up, we tricked your dumb ass." She ran off, then stopped. "Don't dare bring trifling ass to my son's funeral." She spit on the ground in disgust. "I going to pray that the Champ kills you next week."

Then she was gone.

I couldn't think of anything nasty to say in return, so I tried not to look silly, going round and round in a circle. I stood

168

there alone, shivering in my rage. I reluctantly pressed both hands to either side of my head to temporarily harness my fury.

The elegant man honked his horn twice. I followed the sound, saw him waving at me, and became increasingly more furious. So he was the genius who had placed the bounty of fatherhood on my head even when he knew how much it was against my wishes. What gave him the right to make such an appraisal of my young life and estimate that I could use a bastard child in it? I had given myself to him on that night so long ago under the pretense that he would assist me, not make an ass of me.

The elegant man had toyed with my life one time too many, and now I had no doubts about what I was going to do to him.

He blew the horn again. I headed towards the Caddy at easy trot. He smiled, and I smiled back. In no time at all, I was going to shatter his life of comfort and ease, and all the tricks in the world wouldn't be able to fix his little, red wagon.

"Don't tread on me," I whispered to myself as I got into the car. DON'T TREAD ON ME!

6

<u>*This was it!*</u>
<u>*The Night!*</u>

My small, cramped dressing room bristled with electrified adrenaline, and from where I sat, patiently getting my hands wrapped and taped, I could see the atmosphere continuing to boil. Everyone was absorbed totally in the red-hot, white heat of the moment. The walls sweated.

I felt emotionally drugged, but since I kept all my anxieties buttoned up, I appeared less cheerful than the others; however, I, too, was there, locked body and soul into an invisible, primitive netherworld.

This was the quiet rattle and hum of war getting ready to happen, but that wasn't it. Despite how standard and ordinary everything appeared to be, and even though, no one remarked about it, or hinted at it, many, if not all, were already looking ahead to the 'exalted state" that would be ushered in after the fight. I refused to think ahead. I couldn't get past the reality of how menacing the champion looked this evening, how ready he appeared to be to defend that which I had come to deprive him of.

I had to take him. Had to. And it was imperative that I do so under my own authority. I couldn't get hit, couldn't get hurt, or else the elegant man would sabotage the fight. I didn't want that. I wanted to fight a champion, a fully conscious one.

There had never been anything unusual about a fighter abandoning his original fight plan and improvising in the ring from round to round as it suited him no matter how much his corner detested it. Tonight, I would simply add another chapter to the saga.

Now that the moment was full upon me, I did experience an anxious chill. I had trained under duress, thumbing my way through the daily sessions, knowing that I was not going to follow that regimen once I physically faced the champion and the opening bell sounded. At that moment, I would go on a boxing spree to kill or be killed.

Coming into the dressing room, the white-haired gentleman looked a bit of a mess. At last, the mental wear and tear of the moment, and what it meant to The Talented Xth had simply fatigued him. He came over, the elegant man at his elbow.

"How do you feel, Champ?"

"Fantastic," I replied curtly.

"Wonderful," the white-haired gentleman explained. "You were born for this moment."

"Well, let me do it my way. Let me fight without the fear-- ---."

One word from the elegant man and the room was cleared. "We don't have time to go through this again," he growled. "As long as you're fighting your fight and there's no danger, then there will be nothing to fear, but if there is the first sign of any serious trouble----."

"Yeah, yeah, yeah," I shot back angrily. "I know the drill."

"As long as you think you're the best," the white-haired gentleman asked, "why should it matter what anyone else thinks?"

I laughed bitterly. "Get out. Both of you."

"No," the white-haired gentleman stated firmly. "Not until it is once again clear to you how earth-shattering tonight is."

"I know. I know," I responded sternly. "You have bored holes into my head with it for as long as I can recall."

"Be clear about it then. After tonight, no one dare laugh at us because we are different. After tonight, little gay boys will

171

no longer be exempted from being Boy Scouts, and gay teachers will not be ousted from their jobs. Your winning tonight will guarantee that new laws be written that forbids discrimination against homosexuals. Is all this clear to you?"

"Yes," I sighed. "It's clear."

"Then go out there and put on a good show."

I exploded in anger. "There it goes again. The implication that this is no more than a circus act, that I'm nothing but a freak in a carnival."

"That's tough shit," the white-haired gentleman growled, "and it's too damn late to get cold feet, so it's business as usual. You remember your speech?"

The elegant man answered for me. "He'd better."

"Leave me alone, please," I mumbled.

The pair thundered out of the dressing room.

Once alone, I laughed with insane delight. Cheerfully, I reminded myself that I was going to fight my fight out there tonight and I was going to win. Moments later, my entourage trooped back in, and immediately the small, cramped room was again pulsing with raw energy. I fed off the highly-charged electric atmosphere until, at length, I was fortified with high-voltage adrenaline.

One of my trainers sat down next to me. "You ready to be Champeen?"

Before I could answer, a mighty roar went up from outside, deep in the arena. Something had happened, and everyone froze, wondering. There was a knock at the door.

"Kid couldn't get up for the count. Fight's over, so you're next. Get ready."

My mouth suddenly went desert dry as my heartbeat became irregular and my arms turned to dead weight.

"This is it," someone shouted. "All hail the Champ!"

I sounded very small. "Let's finish this."

Instantly, hands were all over me, massaging me, kneading my muscles; loosening me up.

"Dance, champ, dance. Work up a little sweat."

I circled the room, snorting like a horse, throwing jabs.

"Beautiful, baby. Fantastic."

Another knock on the door. Same voice. "Fighter up."

Someone pulled the gloves on, and someone else slipped the black satin robe onto my shoulders. Everyone patted me on the back, wishing me well.

"Let's roll," I ordered.

I was plainly anxious to get to the ring now because it was a familiar place, a sort of comfort zone. Sliding through the ropes would be like a 'welcome home' door-mat too me, and I would automatically be soothed by the tranquility of being in my element.

I danced out of the dressing room, leaning lightly on the shoulders of my lead man, who moved me steadily toward the ring. Upon seeing me, the challenger, a great noise erupted from the sell-out crowd. I ignored the clatter. I saw the ring and thought it a destination too far. I tapped on my trainer lightly on the right shoulder, urging him to go faster, but he patiently continued his controlled pace.

Cameras flashed in the darkened cavern, lighting it up as though the sun had crashed through the roof. Men......boys......women dashed out of their seats to touch or to pat me as I moved slowly down the aisle. Distractedly, I approved of their celebration. That pleased me greatly. At the bottom of the ring, I scrambled swiftly up the steps, but instead of stepping through the ring ropes, I pitched myself them headlong, tucking my body in, somersaulting, then rolling across the canvas only to spring up agilely on the other side, throwing a dazzling array of punches.

The crowd went bananas!

Bravo! Bravo!

Then, another deafening cheer went up from the masses and all attention was suddenly diverted from me. The Champ was making his way to the ring. He came along as a much faster pace as if he didn't have a second to waste. He was all business-like, precise. Despite myself, I watched his approach. I was galvanized by his sure, fluid stride, the loose way his muscles looked, gleaming darkly through his open boxing robe. I became hypnotically riveted, mesmerized by the hard, cold glint in his eyes, the menacing way his black shiny, bald head bobbed up and down on his massive shoulders.

He took the corner opposite me, and immediately tattooed the air with a million punches, beads of his icy sweat falling upon the canvas marking his territory as surely as a dog marks his turf by pissing at a fire hydrant. I understood. Clearly.

He glanced at me to see if I had perceived the threat, and when assured that I had, he went to his corner for any last instructions from his team.

Both our corners became beehives of frantic activity.

"Do this!"

"Don't do that!"

"Remember!

"Forget!

"WIN!"

When the referee called us out to the center of the ring, The Champ pressed his face to within inches of mine. He bared his teeth around his mouthpiece, making a ugly, plastic snarl. His face was stone.

"Hello," I muttered.

He appeared ready to pounce on me then.

All the preliminaries completed, we trotted easily back to our respective corners to await the bell. Time could not have passed any slower, but during the interval, I managed to shut everything out. I had to focus, to concentrate; to be without distraction. Most importantly, I couldn't get staggered. In such an event, I could already envision the panic on the white-haired gentleman's face, exhorting the elegant man to give the signal---- whatever it was----to drug the opponent.

But I wasn't going to permit that to happen. Not tonight. I was going to beat the champion and I was going to do it fair and square. And quickly.

I rushed instantly to the middle of the ring. Seeing that I had reached this psychic nerve center first, the champion held back, dancing prettily on his toes, beckoning me to him. I accepted the challenge. I advanced. I shot off two quick jabs which missed. He responded with a quick, wicked left hook that barely connected. The crowd roared.

I slid inside and began pummeling his midsection with hard lefts and even harder rights. He tried to swing his body out of the way, but I continued to connect, smashing his ribs severely. The crowd cheered.

He took a step back. I followed him and without advance warning, rose from my crouch and fired off a pair of devastating hooks that snapped his head violently from side to side, but he gave no sign of being hurt. Next, his hands exploded through the air with speed I could scarcely calculate, and he hit me three times square on the chin, forcing me back, though, only slightly. He hit me a fourth time, and at once pain flashed throughout the back of my head, seeming to snap something inside my skull, but despite the stars in my eyes, I remained firm on my feet, afraid to move, lest my legs betray me. I couldn't appear dazed.

He punched me in the stomach so hard that it knocked me back a few feet. He pounced inside, but before he could swing again, I grabbed him, hugging tightly. He took this very badly, the grabbing, so he wrestled me off, bouncing a stinging left hook off my jaw in the process. Then he swung six more times as hard as he could.

One by one, I countered each blow, lunging at him on the last punch, putting the full weight of my body behind it. I missed. I was momentarily thrown off balance and he took advantage of my disequilibrium by jabbing twice at my face. I was hit on each occasion, but the damage was minimal.

I hurled a wild, glancing right cross at him on my way back around to face him, and he snapped my head back with a hard, crushing left jab. He hit me in the stomach and I smashed a brutal uppercut under his chin as payback. The crowd was out of their seats.

In a tumultuous exchange, we traded another series of savage punches. I held my ground. He gave no quarter. The massive crowd was intoxicated with mad joy. I pounded a short hook off his head. Then, a second one.

There was pandemonium in the arena!

With a sweeping motion of my feet, I side-stepped his next barrage of punches and was able to land another hook. This time, he clenched. I stuck both my gloves in his chest, shoving hard. He flew backwards, half-turning and stumbling, losing his balance. He was still spinning, placing one foot behind the other, alternatively, attempting to compose himself. Back and forth, his feet went, trying to secure him, but I was there before they could provide him much of a steady brace. A double-barreled pair of hooks put him down.

The crowd was delirious!

He was up quickly, and as soon the ref resumed the contest, he came at me, his lightning fast hands only blurs as he rattled off a succession of hooks and jabs. I absorbed them, being painfully patient; waiting.

This time when he swung, it was at empty space. I was down under the blow. I went to his gut. He gasped. I slid a powerful uppercut, just between his gloves, up the length of his sweaty body, crashing it under his chin. He rose an inch off the floor. Still standing, he tottered on weakened knees, a look of bewilderment in his startled eyes, but one punch later, he was out like a light.

It was over! At 2:41 of the first round, I had finished him to become the new heavyweight champion of the world. But it still wasn't official-----yet.

Bedlam reigned supreme!

Moments later, I stood again in center ring. The wild insanity still raged, followed by the quiet disbelief of what had just happened. The enormous crowd shifted its attention to the ring announcer as he reached for the distended microphone, blowing into it to still the crowd noise. Carefully, he pulled it towards him, started to speak into it, then backed away from it, shaking his head slowly as in shock. He cast a studied glance at me, then at my defeated opponent, surprise still visible on his face.

He needed to say something quick, but whatever it was that he had rehearsed seemed to be the wrong thing to say at the moment. At last, he made up his mind.

"Ladies and gentlemen," he enunciated clearly, "winner by a knockout in two minutes and forty one seconds of the first round, we have a new heavyweight CHAMPION of the world!"

The thunderous applause drowned out everything else he said. Still badly shaken, the ring announcer handled the championship belt with tender care. Then he passed it on to me.

I valiantly held the glittering belt high over my head until the applause died down, and then with a casual toss of my hand, I flung the belt across the ring. It skidded across the canvas as a deathly quiet erupted. Everyone grew hushed and frozen.

From somewhere among the many pair of eyes that bored holes into me, I could specifically feel those of the white-haired gentleman and the elegant man. I angrily snatched the microphone towards me. It swiveled easily until it was only a few inches from my lips. The quiet was immense.

"Ladies and gentlemen of the world," I barked defiantly. "I renounce the heavyweight championship of the world even though I have clearly demonstrated that I am worthy and deserving of it. The title means nothing to me and it would be beneath my dignity to claim it, or to accept it." I paused to catch my breath. "I cannot accept the championship because I'm no champion. I'm a fa-------."

Everyone waited, hanging on to my every word. The suspense was heart-stopping.

"I am no champion," I repeated, "I'm a FAILURE! All those days and nights in the gym training for this one moment turned into years that made me turn my back on, and to neglect my dead son. I failed him. I failed myself and I will fight no more........forever."

Now, I had to run for my life. Or else.

On my way out of the ring, a trusted member of my entourage secretly slipped a piece of party napkin into my hand and squeezed it closed. I got the message. The note was for my eyes only.

I took a quick shower and once we were in the car, I asked the trainer about the address. He merely grunted. "Let's go see." Mumbling, he cast a worried look out of the window. "This should be interesting."

Apparently, we were already in the vicinity of the address because we arrived there quickly, but when we got there, the party was already in full swing. We were met at the door by an individual I had met earlier in the evening before I had been carted off to the secret conference.

"They're here," he yelled over his shoulder. Evidently, everyone was expecting us. "Right this way."

Without fanfare, the music ceased and the revelry came to an immediate halt. In a flash, the complete demeanor of the atmosphere changed, growing intense.

"Welcome, Miss Thang," the host said cordially, kissing me on both cheeks. "So glad you decided to make it." He rolled his big, brown eyes at the trainer. "And why does trouble always have to follow great beauty?"

"Why are we here?" the trainer snapped. "Explain that."

"The reason we are here," the host began, "is because-----
."

"There always has to be a plan B." It was the white-haired gentleman, who had miraculously conjured himself up from out of what had just a second ago been nothingness. He smiled sadistically. "I'm disappointed with you."

That fact hadn't escaped my attention.

"So this is all about, what shall we call it------payback?" The elegant man stared at me coldly. "Why did you cross us, you snot-nosed, red punk?"

Sensing my own demise, I ran up away. I attacked some steps at the back of the hallway like my life depended on it because it did. I took another step. *Up.*

Halfway to the top, I found myself firmly agreeing with the notion that I was very nervous about what might await me up there, but despite the intensity of the danger that going up there induced in me, I felt somewhat courageous that I was strong-willed enough to keep climbing.

UP!

My fingers twitched and felt tingly, and I was ill at ease, but I was only two steps from the top. I fiddled with my nerves one last time and crossed the threshold at the top landing.

And there he was!

I felt the bullets plunge into my chest like scalding balls of fire, the impact and velocity knocking my feet from under me, lifting me up and pitching me back down the stairs I had just ascended. I tumbled backwards over the steps in a thundering roar, my feet, then my head, bouncing loudly against the polished wood. When I hit the bottom, I didn't try to get up. I couldn't. I was down for the count.

The trainer dropped the gun and looked at the elegant man.

"*Long   Live   The   Talented   Xth!*"

Two weeks later, I was secretly whisked out of a private, government hospital by the FBI, and relocated to one of their safe houses in the mountains of Tennessee.

I was confined to a wheelchair, but had no difficulty getting around the spacious three-roomed cabin. The place was well-appointed, and had been redone in my favorite color. The refrigerator and pantry were both stocked to the brim with all of my cherished foods.

The feds knew how to treat a girl!

It all began to make good sense to me now, and there were times when I wondered why this wonderful idea hadn't penetrated my consciousness earlier. Anyway, I loved the idea now. I was impressed with the way I had thought everything out. I smiled. There would be fireworks, but that's what life was all about, wasn't it?

I was going to be splendid. I wanted big breasts, at least 36s. I would get my eyebrows arched, have my long, red legs tapered and shaped, and get all body hair permanently removed by the best surgeon this side of the Mississippi. What else, I thought?..........*My ass!* But what more could be done to it since it was already perfect.

<u>Damn, I was going to be even more beautiful than Mother!</u>

If, by chance, you enjoyed this book, then, by all means, check out my other novels. You can also follow my blog. www.soulfirebooks.com

GIBRAN TARIQ

BETWEEN FIRES

Gibran Tariq

ONE FOOT in the GRAVE